OUTLINES OF MODERN LIBRARIANSHIP

Music librarianship

Malcolm Jones

CLIVE BINGLEY LONDON

K G SAUR   MUNICH · NEW YORK · PARIS

FIRST PUBLISHED 1979 BY CLIVE BINGLEY LTD
SET IN 11 ON 12 POINT BASKERVILLE BY ALLSET
PRINTED AND BOUND IN THE UK BY
REDWOOD BURN LTD TROWBRIDGE AND ESHER
COPYRIGHT © MALCOLM JONES
ALL RIGHTS RESERVED
ISBN 085157-274-X

Clive Bingley Ltd
Commonwealth House
New Oxford Street, London WC1

K G Saur Verlag
Postfach 71 10 09
D-8000 Munich 71

K G Saur Publishing Inc
175 Fifth Avenue
New York, NY 10010

K G Saur Editeur
38 rue de Bassano
F-75008 Paris

British Library Cataloguing in Publication Data

Jones, Malcolm
    Music librarianship. - (Outlines of
    modern librarianship; 5).
    1. Music libraries
    I. Title   II. Series
    026'. 78   ML111

    ISBN 0-85157-274-X

Music
librarianship

OUTLINES OF MODERN LIBRARIANSHIP

Titles included in the series are

Children's librarianship
Local studies librarianship
Special librarianship
Book production
Library history
Current awareness services
Cataloguing
Music librarianship
History and theory of classification
Practical reference work
Public library administration
Medical librarianship

CONTENTS

INTRODUCTION

Members of the United Kingdom Branch of the International Association of Music Libraries will surely welcome this book. Malcolm Jones has provided an excellent survey of the work they do as music librarians in all kinds of library. It is particularly to be commended for its balanced approach to the relationship between music librarianship and the wider professions of which it forms a part. It is to be hoped that librarians generally will therefore find it a useful text by which to come to an understanding of what their colleagues in music libraries are trying to do.

Miriam Miller
President
IAML (UK)

PREFACE

THIS BOOK was written with two intentions in mind. First, I wanted to shew to those who have some interest in music libraries from an outside viewpoint—librarian colleagues in other specialities or none, and musicians who are sympathetic to work libraries try to do for them—a general view of what music libraries are about and can do, and possibly to clear up some misconceptions.

The second intention was to provide those who are beginning a study of the subject with a kind of small scale chart of the whole territory, both to give a clearer idea of its general shape, and the interrelation of its parts, and to lead on to larger scale maps, and to indicate points of departure.

I am well aware that members of the first group have been, and doubtless will continue to be, drafted into music librarianship, full or part time; and I hope to make the process a little easier, while also providing for those beginning a special study of a field which merits singleminded study. It is curious and unfortunate that in an area as small as music librarianship, the subdivisions—especially into research libraries, performance libraries, sound recording libraries and so on—should be so keenly felt; and I believe that, even when working in institutions that are primarily one of these kinds, a librarian gives a better service for some awareness of the other complementary elements of the field. Even in public libraries, which most of all should be balanced and integrated, one can think of many that have overemphasised one of these aspects.

Although I have argued that the intending music librarian should have acquired a basic musical knowledge, but more importantly an attitude to music, before embarking on library

9

study, I realise how often this has not been possible. I have therefore explained some problems about the nature of music which may seem painfully obvious to those who are brought daily into forceful contact with them. Similarly, the professional librarian will find some of the basic assumptions of his trade spelt out. Given the dual nature of the intended readership, this seemed inevitable and, if it is too disingenuous to suggest that awareness of the often unspoken assumptions of daily life is salutary, then some paragraphs had better be skipped from time to time.

Acknowledgments
In a general outline of a subject there is likely to be little that is very original. If the ingredients are not too new I can only hope the presentation is tolerable, being aware that among colleagues and friends are those who know much more on any particular area. The list of my creditors is, therefore, large; and to single out individuals would be invidious. If I have any of that attitude to music for which I have argued as the *sine qua non* of the music librarian, I owe it most of all to early experience, especially in the music department of the University of Southampton, where the daily mental stimulus is as vivid a memory after a decade and a half as it was on leaving. Music librarians are mostly gregarious, and to those who have taken me in to their libraries and explained their methods, my thanks.

Much is discussed when we gather at meetings and conferences, and although the effects may not be seen immediately, a good deal sinks into the pot to emerge much later; and many of my friends in IAML, especially in the UK branch and its executive committee, may recognise the piece they tossed in. On either side of any librarian stand the retail trade (wherein good friends should, following Polonius, be grappled to the soul with hoops of steel) and I owe much to some good friends there; and the public, among whom individuals may be delightful or distracting, but for whose benefit it all takes place, and from whom we learn all the time.

To all my colleagues in Birmingham Public Libraries, and especially the staff of the music library, I owe a debt whose extent only they can measure, and I gratefully acknowledge it.

The opportunity to create a new music library comes to few of us, and is as good a teacher in its way as the need to give the best on limited resources. The last few years have seen us trying to do both. The whole view, and any particular parts of it, is my responsibility and, while acknowledging these debts, any errors of fact or imbalances of judgement remain my own.

I am grateful to Alan Pope, who read some chapters in type-script and made helpful suggestions, and to Lesley Leigh who typed from my unattractive manuscript at great speed. Especially my debt is to Frances, my wife, who has suffered not only the writing of this, but my absence from the home and family she has been left to manage, while gathering information. As a practising musician (always short of practice time) she has been involved in the process; I hope it was worthwhile.

September 1978

ONE

MUSIC LIBRARIES AND THOSE THEY SERVE

THERE IS no typical library or library user, and the range of music libraries, or music sections of libraries, is wider than most. In a book on sources of information in music, J H Davies divided the chapters by kinds of musicians, from the ordinary listener through three kinds of conductors, four of performers, then the educator, the musicologist and so on to fourteen chapters. Many users of the public library regard the music department as just the collection of recordings for loan, and rarely, if ever, use any other facility. To library administrators, the music library may be a source of friction in a well-oiled routine, having custody of special kinds of materials, raising special problems for most housekeeping routines and making special pleading when policy is under discussion.

Those who work in music libraries, whether they are in charge of a collection of international significance, or look after a music collection in a small general library as a part of other duties, or give a service to a more specialist institution, are aware of these problems and have found some working arrangements for the day to day chores. Whatever their training and experience, they will need to have some involvement with music, and especially the musical life of at least some part of the community they serve. Music lovers have a jargon and an abbreviated way of talking: if they can ask for Boult's Planets or Abba's new album without having to spell it out and be understood, their confidence will be the greater.

Few of those who have become distinguished music librarians chose that course on leaving school and pursued it singlemindedly thereafter. There is an old controversy on the relative usefulness of musical training and library training in a music library. Clearly the ideal is to have both. To those

13

thinking of their own future, it is my opinion that the basics of library and bibliographic skills can be taught in a reasonably short time; but those with neither knowledge of, nor interest in, music are likely to be unhappy and little use in a music library. Deep knowledge of music or some part of it, while valuable, is not necessary; extensive rather than intensive musical experience and an inquiring frame of mind is the basis needed. The training of music librarians will be returned to in a later chapter; it should be said though that, in spite of the minor frustrations and the fact that there is no solution to some of the problems which will be discussed, music librarianship can be very satisfying. The reasons perhaps have to do with music more than libraries. Music librarians feel some special kinship and sometimes find themselves separated from the mainstream of library work. This must not be exaggerated; most of what is true about library management generally, holds in music libraries; and too much special pleading weakens any case. Yet it must be said that the physical nature of printed music, no less than recordings, raises some problems which do not occur to those without direct experience of them. The vital difference, however, is not in these physical factors, large though they loom to those who handle the material, but in the nature of the musical experience itself.

Music exists only as it is created and recreated in sound and time; and those who work in aspects of music removed from its performance, seem to feel a need to be involved in performance from time to time—as if to assert what it is they are really about. So it can be argued that the music librarian's daily work is juxtaposed to that of the performer, more nearly than his colleague who passes written information to the seeker for knowledge, by the very imprecision of the printed page of music compared to that of the book. This is true at all levels of performing skill: in giving a teenager the sheet music for a current pop song, so that he can pick it out on a guitar, or supplying a professional orchestra. The librarian's choice of edition may affect the performance, the choice of stock may, indeed, determine which pieces will be performed; and a willingness to take part in communication on these subjects, contributing from professional knowledge, is a vital asset for a music librarian, as well as a source of much satisfaction.

14

It is not surprising, then, that the performer is considered first in most surveys of music consumers. The tendency to put performance first has been strengthened of late, at least in Western Europe. Schools teach more performers than previously; amateur music making shows no decline, even in the face of a technology which makes the sounds of the world's best performers available to all; and the musicologist has notably espoused the performer, a union which is bearing fruit.

The prime service of the music library, and that most frequently required of it, is to make music, printed or recorded, available to the user, and a high proportion of the demands which users make, whether or not expressed to the librarian, is for specific works. The more easily the seeker can find, the better the library; however congenial the personal contact between librarian and client, it means a less speedy end to the search than might have been. It is only when the client is less clear about his need or less able to formulate it, that the wider and deeper aspects of the librarian's knowledge are called for.

Kinds of libraries
Within the accepted division of libraries into public, academic and special, the public librarian clearly faces the whole range of users—this is at once his greatest joy and burden. Variety is surely the spice of life; but a wide range of need, indeed of uncertainty of future need, makes anticipation and provision especially difficult. On the other hand, public music librarians are part of larger library systems, and the general policy and much of the practice of administration will be quite above their control. This still allows initiative, but at least puts it in a framework.

The academic library will serve some institution: university, college or school, with a much more limited community having a considerable measure of common purpose. The bulk of the work undertaken by students will be reasonably predictable, and will largely recur from generation to generation. Research staff may be expected to plan and predict, and will probably have some narrowly defined areas of special interest. Here, more than in public libraries, librarians with sensitivity to their clients and good communications can see immediate short-term rewards, as well as the strategic, long-term ones that any librarian will find.

In the category of special music libraries comes a wide range of size: major national, even international collections assume responsibilities to their colleagues in the profession as well as to their users, and become both places of last resort and leaders of professional practice. While those with smaller resources may envy them, they are particularly subject to pressure, often very well-informed and loudly expressed, but sometimes contradictory, and their practices are exposed to a wide view. On the other hand, the librarians of orchestras, choral societies, opera houses and the like, have an all too predictable need; and they are expected to fulfil it unerringly and immediately, whether or not the materials can be had. Here there may be less reliance on one's own collection and more on obtaining material from outside it for special needs; although most such libraries are well advised to build and maintain a collection if they can, if only in self-protection against future non-availability or price inflation.

Planning the library

It is, of course, very unlikely that the first experience of anyone in music librarianship will be of planning a library, and many go through an entire career without doing so. The pattern is much more likely to be of starting in an existing, working library, probably in a rather junior capacity. Nevertheless the objectives and plan of a library merit constant reconsideration; and all who are involved can contribute, and should be encouraged to do so. Thus it is worth considering planning without any preconceptions, and in more modern styles of management there may be scope for involvement of all staff. Just as a house buyer may acquire no garden but an empty plot of land, or one with an overgrown wilderness, and then plan a garden, preferably indoors in winter, and work towards the plan in the coming years, so the library may have to grow slowly toward what is planned. There will be no winter or armchair, however, for the librarian, who must plan while giving what service is possible; but the experience of standing back and looking is valuable. A successful plan requires experience, and the ability to see the library with the user's eye, and should include as much knowledge as can be gathered— often fairly blatantly, by visiting other libraries and talking to

16

their staff. Most professional groups, both student and practising, are inveterate visitors to their colleagues.

If the scope of the users is defined as far as possible, the next question is: what resources, particularly of money and personnel, are available? This may be illogical—one should ask what services should be provided *first*, then what level of resources would sustain it; but no institution has infinite resources, and in fact, most will lay down the level fairly clearly from the start. Thereafter, there is some small scope for discussion.

Many music libraries are housed in buildings that were intended for quite different purposes: warehouses, chapels and shops, for example. Imagination and a clear view of the needs has sometimes done wonders, and the result can be instructive. Some purpose-built libraries, planned with less of these qualities, especially where the special requirements of music are concerned, may be less so. All the kinds of material to be kept, and any equipment necessary for their storage and use, must be considered; and their relative quantities, initially and after some decades, estimated. The kinds of use each will engender may be very different: record borrowers will happily browse standing up, while those who wish to consult the collected works of, say, Schoenberg will want to sit with these large volumes on a table, and probably use other material simultaneously—a notepad, another score, perhaps a gramophone and records; they will also be much less tolerant of extraneous noise.

Staff will need space on two counts at least, each member having a place that will not be disturbed by others; but some housekeeping processes, particularly of acquisition, cataloging, issue and so on requiring their own area where whoever is working on that task will go. A change in practice, such as that from card catalogue to book catalogue, or microform, can have far reaching implications on space needed. So can the need for an extra set of shelves, or browser of records. Can matching equipment be obtained? All equipment, in particular, is likely to last a shorter time than the building, and in drawing up a list of equipment needed and the place of each item, possible changes may be guessed at and catered for if possible, or their use not prevented altogether—perhaps by omitting electric supply in a major area.

17

Maybe the library will put on exhibitions and displays—
perhaps even concerts. The planner, having considered all
that must be accommodated, must next consider their interrelation, all human activities as far as possible being considered
as movement and stations on the plan. All this must be clear
before the taste of the designer, amateur or professional, can
start to act on the whole to produce a pleasant and attractive
environment. It will not be so if some aesthetic preconception
is allowed to override the plan. To librarians experienced in
library design, but not in a music library situation, the points
most needing emphasis are the wide variety of physical sorts
of materials—not just the obvious recordings and so on, but
the huge size folios for example, the fact that music is discarded
from stock much less, and the need for acoustic control, not
only of an auditorium (if there is one), but of study areas or
recording rooms.

Budget
If the physical layout of the library is generally a fairly fixed
one, then so too is the budget. Some increases to offset the
inevitable price rises, some cuts when hard times come in,
these are inevitable; but the pattern is rarely of great change.
Most institutions budget on a fixed period, usually the year,
and the librarian has an allowance for the period, usually again
broken down (outside his control) into the various kinds of
expenditure. Thus the argument that extra expense on equipment may reduce staff needed, or at least improve the ef-
ficiency of those there are, may well be impossible to push to
its logical conclusion. The astute librarian will learn ways of
supplementing the allocation in some situations; good publicity may bring in some worthwhile gifts to the stock, and
some fund-raising activities may be permissible.
   The budget underlies all other planning, whether on a capital or a recurring basis, and however inadequate and immut-
able it may seem at any one time, it is as well to consider not
only the objectives of the library, the number of users, regular
and irregular, and the range of demands they will make, but
also their corollaries: the size of stock and rate of expansion
of it, the equipment needed to use it fully and the size and
range of personnel needed, and to cost them. This exercise is

salutary, and needs regular reappraisal, since change in objectives and growth of demand can only ever be estimates. Life
is such, however, that the opportunity to represent a pressing
need may come quite unexpectedly, and it is well to be in full
command of such facts, along with supporting statistics.

Acquisition policy
Most librarians will agree on the need for some statement of
policy on acquisition, especially in a field like music, where
the range of material and subject is wide. One may suspect,
however, that the number who put this into practice is smaller.
The policy will start with consideration of the relevance of
each area to the users of that library. If the library is part of
a larger whole, then many responsibilities will already be defined. It may be a useful rule of thumb to divide the budget
between books, music and recordings—even if the financial
administration does not insist on separate heads of account
for these items. Further subdivision, as a guide, may be helpful. In some areas the annual size of output and cost are available, and this is a great help in determining what scale of purchase is feasible.

Most general libraries will require a representative collection of music of all times and from all places, including the
significant composers, forms of composition and performance
media. Having attempted all representatively, they will probably cover a narrower range of time and place, related to their
own, more comprehensively. For many libraries in Europe,
this will mean the European 'classical' tradition of the last
four or five centuries, and the fund of available music is clearly
largest in this area. One might doubt the wisdom of such a
bias in a new library in Asia, for example, even though it can
be observed in fact. But the librarian may feel it a duty to
'support' areas less well known and researched; earlier music,
or some contemporary folk or popular traditions for example.
Demand, both from the general public and the specialist, is
noticeably more catholic than hitherto, and some library attitudes of twenty years ago now seem rather condescending.

Having put the subject areas first, it is then necessary to
consider the forms which materials take. This is often dic-
tated by the use to which they will be put, and thus again a

study of users determines policy. A town with no orchestra needs no sets of orchestral performance material. One needs particularly though to watch for specious distinctions by form; how do libraries with sheet music of pop songs justify not having pop records? Some areas raise particular problems which the library may not have the resources to deal with: orchestral and chamber music performance material, programme notes, instrumental tutors, are examples. It is easy to assume that because a demand for a particular category is not expressed across the library counter, it does not exist. Only a librarian who participates in the community's musical activity and is familiar with its performing life, across the wider spectrum, and the courses of study offered, can see deficiencies in the stock. There is often a vicious circle constraining the repertory, especially of amateur groups, to playing music that is known because it is easily available, and a valuable service of the librarian is to widen such repertories. As between one work and another there is no absolute standard, and the temptation may be to play safe, especially as regards lesser known works. Only the least experienced should place much reliance on published 'basic repertory guides' or the like; these are notoriously subject to fashions of time and place, as a glance at a twenty-year old example will show. Far better to cultivate sensitivity to the current fashion, while learning, even at the cost of some mistakes, to back one's own judgment on the lasting value. Heaviest demand must be heeded, but not to the exclusion of other factors.

Much music will remain in the library for a very long time compared with books (short of loss or wear), and in the acquisition of music, libraries show very much less emphasis on the current output of publishers than with books. This means that whereas two libraries in similar situations will have many book titles in common in their acquisitions over a given period, this will not be so of music. This is perhaps the main reason why co-operation over acquisitions between libraries has been less in evidence in music, but where the possibilities exist, particularly in the fields of periodicals and some expensive works in series, collected editions and the like, they can be worthwhile. This may be especially valuable where two libraries serving somewhat different communities are geographically close—a public library and a university library in the same town for example. It may be possible to co-operate over the more expensive and less regularly used reference and bibliographic tools, especially where these partially duplicate each other.

Much of the standard repertory is available in several editions, and in recordings of a number of different performances. The extent to which more than one of these should be acquired, at the cost perhaps of not having any copy of some lesser works, is a policy matter. Some editions and performances attract different kinds of users, and where such differing demands are encountered, it may be well to satisfy them; consider a young beginner pianist and a harpsichordist expert in the performance of the French baroque school both requiring a Couperin piece; or a recording of the St Matthew Passion suitable for a Bach scholar and one for a local (English) church's Lent devotional meeting. In the case of recordings, there has been even less co-operation on acquisitions, even among libraries who accept the principle when applied to books; and the expectations aroused in the few schemes have not been fulfilled. Perhaps the unevenness of provision is a factor; there is also less commitment to the recording in libraries, which makes it vulnerable at times of stress and constraint.

One other area where policy must be thought out, before practical considerations complicate the issue, is anthologies. Much popular music is issued in albums, which are especially attractive to the amateur. On the other hand, the editing and presentation often are less satisfactory; and the album is difficult to place in the library and to catalogue. Some public libraries have browsing collections (uncatalogued) of such material, arguing that titles are to be found elsewhere in the main collection for the 'serious' user. This can be a useful compromise, especially for piano music and songs, for a library with sufficient resources to allow the duplication. The principle is that duplication must always be deliberate, not only in each specific case, but as a matter of policy in view of the differing needs that each copy will satisfy. One other kind of anthology which is in a class of its own is the collection edited with a pedagogic intent. There are some such collections, often covering a particular period or style, with not only good editorial work on text, but also outstanding commentaries on performance practice; and any library serving those who are consciously learning (as most libraries will be) will find these worth having, even at the cost of some material not being found at all.

One other category of material which any library has a special duty to preserve is that with a local connection. Much of this is ephemeral and may not be of high quality, but in such a narrow field this is overridden by the usefulness for the future, if not the present. Manuscripts and scrapbooks from local composers, concert programmes and archives of local societies—such material can often be obtained at relatively little cost by a librarian who has contacts in the community. At the other end of the scale in cost of acquisition is antiquarian material. The cost of even nineteenth century music has risen sharply over the last few years, and few new libraries can hope to compete in a field which is increasingly being left to the largest libraries to cover. Much early material of significance for its subject matter is fortunately available in reprint. However, apart from the interest to historical bibliography, there is something to be said for allowing modern musicians the chance to see the physical form music took in other cultures, in order the better to understand the performance problems and practices. How did a seventeenth century group perform from one copy of a Dowland four part ayre? Or a Renaissance lutenist read from the notation known as tablature? These questions are most easily answered with the copy in front of one.

The acquisition policy, then, needs thinking and rethinking apart from the practice of selection and ordering, which is a more complicated matter in the case of music than is often realised by those not directly involved. This practice will be discussed in later chapters dealing separately with music, books and recordings.

Community involvement
Music provides the librarian with a particularly rich source of opportunity for what has been called extension activities, but is now generally seen as an integral part of library

involvement in the community. It is not possible to set out a plan for such work, rather opportunities and initiatives must be taken and seized when they occur. Personal contact is a major factor in making such enterprises possible.

Libraries may themselves promote concerts, live and recorded, and some have a purpose-built auditorium, others using premises not their own. Similarly, talks and lectures, sometimes directly associated with musical events can be arranged. If the community has composers or performers, mutual benefit may be derived from featuring their work, especially if they will be involved in person. There may be festivals, or at least, competitions, providing opportunity for co-operation. A local radio station is an obvious point of contact.

Most libraries attempt some kind of publicity, based on explanatory leaflets and posters and perhaps running to publications of lasting value. Often groups of people will welcome a speaker from the library—not necessarily to talk only on the services it offers. Librarians and libraries have suffered from a stereotyped image in the public mind. The only remedy is for the public to see librarians active in as many ways as, collectively, they can be in the whole community. Thus the barrier can be broken which still prevents some from realising that the library has something to offer them.

TWO

PRINTED MUSIC

THE CORE of a music library is its collection of 'texts', representing all the significant forms of music, whether considered historically, by composers, schools of composition, forms or performing media. However imprecise the notation of music as a means of recording the sound, the medium of recording cannot replace it, coming as it does after the event of performance, which is usually made possible only by the written music. The range of forms printed music may take may seem daunting to the inexperienced; in fact, it is conditioned by the use for which the music is intended. The easiest way to appreciate this is to use it, preferably in a wide range of musical situations; this is why those with such experience are at such an advantage in a music library. Less tractable is the problem of the wide range of alternatives for the same purpose: so much of the standard repertory is available in a bewildering range of alternative editions, whose text may vary but slightly (if significantly) but whose accessory material, editor's notes, performance notes, binding, paper quality and availability are very different. Is duplication desirable or avoidable, and how to avoid expensive mistakes, are problems even for the experienced in a situation which is changing all the time. The two basic problems need examination at greater length.

Printed music is often referred to, for library convenience, as 'scores', or sometimes 'sheet music'. In fact, these are two particular categories in the area. It is probably most convenient to consider music as basically intended either for performance use, or for study without actual performance (the two overlap). In any piece involving more than one performer, there can be separate presentation of the music each performs, each musician getting a 'part' which literally shews his own part in the ensemble and no more; or the total can be presented by writing out each part on the page one above the other, in a conventional order, so that sounds intended to be heard simultaneously are written vertically above one another. This is a 'score'. Some instruments can play more than one part—so a piano piece is really a score comprising the two parts, one each for right and left hand, and an organ three—right and left hands, and feet. Indeed, each hand may play more than one part in a contrapuntal composition such as a fugue. Bach's fugues, for example, are frequently in three or four parts, occasionally five, to be distributed between the fingers of two hands. While all this may seem obvious to the point of impertinence to those who have ever used music, it is only the beginning.

For some reason the convention became established long ago that singers work from scores, but instrumentalists, except pianists in chamber music, from parts. Thus a singer can see what his colleagues are doing, but an orchestral player cannot. However, if there is an orchestral accompaniment to vocal music, the score is for convenience at rehearsal often reduced to retain the vocal parts separately, but with the orchestral accompaniment arranged for piano. This saves the printer space, and allows choirs to rehearse without the expense of the orchestra in the earlier stages. This form of presentation is called a 'vocal score', and is almost always assumed by enquirers after operas and choral works if they are performing them, and often if they are not. For much opera, it is the only form readily available—the full score, with its comprehensive presentation of all instruments, because it is less frequently required, is often not an economic proposition to the publisher to sell. So the single copy on the shelf, and those making up a set for the singers in a choir or opera for example, are identical. But for orchestral or chamber music, there will be both score and parts. Players will need a set of parts, in identical edition, and published and sold as a unit.

They may also want, and the student or concertgoer is most likely to want, a score. Now since a score in such circumstances is held in the hand, and a part put on a music stand, the score can be smaller in format and typesize than

26

the part. In fact, many popular titles are sold in what is known as 'miniature score' form, or 'pocket' or 'study' score forms. A larger score will be required in addition for the orchestral conductor—though he may use a miniature in emergency if his eyesight is good.

The miniature form has become widely available by the happy technical accident of the application of photography to the printing of music. Movable type, as classically used for books, was always complicated and expensive for music. Instead, engraving, and after its invention in the early nineteenth century, lithography, was used. Engraving, by striking into plates with a punch, was particularly well suited to music since it allowed the repetition of the few basic shapes of note in a large variety of positions as is characteristic of musical notation. However, this skill is fast dying out as the photographic processes of the last thirty years allow cheaper work, and in the case of miniature scores, reproduction of the same text as the full score, the reduction in size being effected as part of the photographic process. It also allows the passing off of more or less admitted reprints as new editions, but that is another matter. The distinction between scores and parts is clearest with orchestral material. Instrumental solos are relatively straightforward, and if accompanied, then the accompanist (almost always piano) has a score in which the other instrument is printed, often in smaller type, above the piano part.

Chamber music is conveniently divided first into that with a piano, which has a score, the other instruments having parts, which are slighter. This set of score and parts should always be kept together, as the loss of one invariably means the replacement of the whole. The second sort is a set of parts, there being no piano. Traditionally libraries put the parts of the first in a pocket at the back of the score, while the second has them all enclosed in a slip-case. Larger sets of parts may be kept in large cases, or strong paper envelopes as the budget allows. One more important presentation applies to concertos and similar works. Here, rather similarly to the vocal score, the publisher often issues a reduced score with the orchestra arranged for piano, and a separate solo part. A soloist asking for such a work will want this form, while a concertgoer will often want a miniature score. To make matters worse, the enquirer will often not state the, to him, entirely obvious fact of which use he requires, relying on some kind of telepathy, or at least, deduction from context. The librarian should never fear to ask in such cases; and where the score is not to hand but is being requisitioned in some way, the distinction must be noted, since once the enquirer has left, a further enquiry will have to be made on the point.

These distinctions then, arise out of the need of the user, and are not some kind of special obstacle course for the music librarian. If they seem obvious to the experienced, so too they will to the user of the library (even if not expressed) and the wrong form is as useless to the user as the wrong title.

Most of the distinctions of scores arise (except for the miniature scores) with music intended for performance. Most libraries keep miniature scores separately, both because they serve a separate purpose, and because their size, generally rather smaller in height than an average book, makes it physically convenient. A category of material to be found in the more substantial library is the collected edition, the definitive (or so its editor hoped) text of the works of a composer, with critical commentary and such material. These are generally large in physical size and in price, and are published in series over a considerable time. They are often kept for reference, cheaper and smaller volumes being generally adequate for many performance needs, while they can be consulted to supplement such everyday copies on particular points. The principle extends beyond the collection of one composer, to series of music with some common factor as, for example, nationality. *Musica Britannica*, published by Stainer and Bell in association with the Royal Musical Association is perhaps the most frequently encountered example of the category, often referred to as Denkmäler from the titles of early German examples. Much important music, particularly though not exclusively from before 1750, is to be found only in such collections. Unless one's catalogue lists all the holdings of each volume (and few do) such pieces may be missed. Fortunately there are books which index the contents of such collections, and familiarity with these is necessary. Such series are generally associated with editions for study purposes, but this is not always the case. Although parts are not available for, for example, the original Denkmäler series, where these cover items of chamber music, they are for editions like the new Halle Handel edition and the new edition of Bach.

Some pieces in *Musica Britannica* volumes have been published separately as offprints especially for choirs. There are also series especially intended for performance use: *Nagel's Musikarchiv*, *Hortus musicus* (Bärenreiter of Kassel) and *Diletto musicale* (Doblinger of Vienna) being examples largely in the instrumental music field; while *Das Chorwerk* (Möseler, Wolfenbüttel) is as the title suggests, a series of choral pieces, mostly of the fifteenth to seventeenth centuries and not published elsewhere. For keyboard music there is no problem and an edition like the *Corpus of early keyboard music* (American Institute of Musicology) is useful to player and scholar alike.

When the librarian considers the basic repertory of Western European 'classical' music, he is confronted by a bewildering array of editions; some clearly reflecting different purpose, but many appearing to duplicate one another. The piano sonatas of Beethoven, for example, are currently (mid-1978) available in the UK in at least twenty-two editions, with another half dozen or so, recently out of print, to be found in many libraries. Two collected editions of Beethoven can be discounted: one was published in the last century (although like many of these editions it is reprinted without quoting the source) and the current one is only available as part of the whole of Beethoven's works. At around thirty pounds sterling a volume for the two volumes of sonatas, this edition will not be bought casually or in error. But what of the 'everyday' editions, available in the local shop? Most are of German origin, some claim the authority of a well-known musicologist as textual editor, or pianist as commentator on performance and provider of fingering. To get some idea of the standards required of an editor, one can hardly do better than read Thurston Dart's second chapter in *The interpretation of music* Hutchinson 1954. The basic principle is honesty—giving as far as possible what the composer wrote and distinguishing clearly additions, particularly those that are matters of opinion.

The term 'urtext' has been coined, meaning an edition giving the composer's text shorn of any accretions or additions, but some urtext editions, especially the older ones, are suspect. In any case, it is usually desirable that an editor give variant texts, with some explanation of the reason, and guidance on performance, so long as what is suggested editorially is clearly distinct from any indication the composer gave. This obviously varies from one composer to another: Elgar for example, left meticulous and careful performing directions, and saw his own works through the press of a careful publisher; whereas most baroque works have been edited from manuscripts devoid of all but the notes of the music. The standard of the text should be the first consideration, but the presence of some annotation on the text, or perhaps more important, its performance, will be valued by many users.

The librarian will then consider paper quality and binding, if any, which vary widely, but there may be no alternatives in many cases. Much French music, for example, is presented on poor paper; while the German editions are much better in this respect. The 'feel' of a good edition must be acquired as quickly as possible, and comes largely from putting oneself in the place of the final user, and asking how far it will answer all the questions, large or small, which that user may ask. Many libraries are still content with poor editions, products mostly of the UK and the USA, giving a text which is someone's opinion of what the composer ought to have written (the changes not being specified), without any editorial remarks at all, and a title placing the piece in the vaguest terms: *Minuet* by Purcell, *Rondo* by Mozart or the like. Be especially suspicious of those who claim to know what a classic composer would do in the twentieth century.

Arrangements are a special source of trouble, especially when not described as such. A good arrangement needs as much sensitivity to style as an edition of an original, and one should expect quotation of source as a matter of routine. Baroque music is frequently arranged unsuitably, although the principle of arrangement, or at least transcription (rewriting

30

for another medium) was regular practice at the time. There are some special cases of arrangement, and the purposes seem worthy. First, simply to provide a larger repertoire for instruments not well blessed: one thinks of trombone or bassoon, for example; and allied to this process is the provision of teaching or study material. There has been a substantial increase in the number of school-age performers on woodwind and brass in particular, and publishers, especially in the USA and UK have provided new material, often in the form of arrangements, to fill the need.

An older tradition is that of arranging orchestral works for piano, solo or duet. Such reductions provided the main means whereby earlier generations got to know the symphonic repertory, in an age before sound recordings, and where concertgoing could not be frequent. The availability of the orchestral experience, or something like it, on record, does not render such arrangements superfluous; and the intimate knowledge of the structure of music which comes from hearing and feeling it at once may be seen as complementary to hearing the colour and texture of the original. Such arrangements will, therefore, be for private use rather than public performances. By contrast, the many arrangements of orchestral works for organ, which were intended for public performance, have now fallen into disfavour, along with the whole ethos of romantic orchestral imitation which was characteristic of the nineteenth century and early twentieth, and much of this is in any case out of print.

One cannot always rely on statements made on the title page or cover of a piece of music. Arrangements may be treated as new works; hence, for example, Purcell's suites for the piano or Marcello's trombone sonatas which neither composer actually wrote. Editors sometimes give a completely new title, or use a title so vague, or which occurs so often, as to be useless. We may all know what is meant by Handel's *Largo* (to the composer an aria from the opera *Serse*) but Telemann's *Suite* (he wrote several hundred) or Purcell's *Minuet*, mean nothing.

The librarian must, therefore, always consider carefully both the way music is described on the score, and the way it is described by enquirers. Some idea of the difficulties may be gained by referring to one well known piece, that usually referred to as 'Jesu, joy of man's desiring', by Bach. This is the most frequently encountered English translation of the text Bach set, in German: 'Jesus bleibet meine Freude'. In the original, it is the sixth and tenth movement of the cantata number 147, *Herz und Mund und That und Leben,* and authentic editions of the original will probably be of the complete cantata. However, it has been arranged as an independent piece for a large number of combinations, as the table opposite shews. No one work of reference lists all these, of course, and the table is probably incomplete on compilation— certainly it will shortly become so. A single publisher, Oxford University Press, lists fifty items under this title, each with ISBN. Before leaving the problem it illustrates, it is worth remarking that, where variant translations of a text appear from different publishers, a source of considerable problems even if, as here, all begin with an important word, a clue is often given by the fact that all share the metre of the original, in order to be sung to the same music. Often this is the only way to guess the original from which a title referred to by an enquirer derives. The pitfalls to be borne in mind when ordering music are well summarised in the article by Dawson and Marks, *Brio* 2(1) Spring 1965, 8-10.

Retail supply
Librarians used to the business ethics of the book trade will be surprised to learn how frequently music is bought direct from publishers (both by librarians and the general public) most of whom maintain retail outlets for the purpose. The extreme scarcity of music retailers is clearly related to the fact, though the situation is that of the proverbial chicken and egg. In view of the difficulties of obtaining music, a retailer with a good stock, irrespective of publisher (and therefore including many foreign published titles) and an experienced staff, is of the greatest value to the music librarian. Unfortunately, both these criteria require considerable capital outlay; and the profits which may be expected are smaller, pro rata, than obtained in the book trade. In many countries libraries expect discount on retail price from a bookseller, and, while some music retailers give it,

J S Bach Cantata no 147 Herz und Mund und That und Leben
soloists, chorus and orchestra
Original and complete editions, different physical forms:

Full score	3 editions
Miniature score	2 editions
Orchestral parts	3 editions
Vocal score	3 editions
Choral score	2 editions

Chorale, usually entitled 'Jesu, joy of man's desiring.'
(3 other English translations), published separately (also frequently in albums), arranged for:
Voices with piano accompaniment
- (1) unison
- (2) 2-part
- (3) female choir
- (4) male choir
- (5) 4-part (as original) 5 editions, and in tonic sol-fa notation

Song (6) solo voices with piano accompaniment, 3 editions 2 different keys.

Instrumental ensemble, score and parts
- (7) recorders
- (8) string trio
- (9) string orchestra
- (10) brass
- (11) orchestra   3 editions
- (12) school orchestra 2 editions

- (13) jazz ensemble

Instruments solo
- (14) piano solo   13 editions
- (15) piano duet   2 editions
- (16) two pianos   10 editions

- (17) organ   17 editions

Instrument with piano accompaniment
- (18) violin
- (19) viola
- (20) cello
- (21) flute
- (22) clarinet
- (23) oboe
- (24) trumpet

*Table to illustrate the many forms that may be taken
by one musical 'title'.*

the music librarian must expect to find it at least reduced in the case of more difficult items.

The trend among book retailers for the more competitive to offer many forms of servicing, the costs of which may be either a direct charge on the purchasers, or free, or related to the rate of discount, is evident among a few music retailers. These services may be seen as either providing knowledge or providing manual labour. Under the first head the experienced retailer is, because of regular contact with publishers, better aware of the current situation in a very fluid market; and he can guide on availability and relative merit of different editions, as well as being able to obtain foreign publications at the cheapest source. Retailers can often obtain catalogues more readily from publishers than can librarians. They may also produce catalogues of their own, though these generally omit publisher information, presumably to try to avoid direct dealing between librarian and publisher. In fact, it is unlikely to do so where a librarian is determined to trade thus, and is very irritating to others.

Although some forms of direct dealing are likely to continue, the practice inevitably puts pressure on the retailers, whose disappearance would be devastating to music purchasers. A very few retailers operate approval order services, or blanket orders, where all or a selection of items within certain predetermined categories are supplied. As far as the manual processes are concerned, the increase in provision of library stationery, jacketing and so on, so noticeable with books, is not evident with music; nor, surprisingly, is the sale of material already bound to library standards very general. A service which combines both professional and manual skill is the provision of catalogue entries. Although several gramophone record suppliers have notably provided this service, it is rare for music; but its advantages, especially for smaller libraries, are considerable.

Publishing
The number of music publishers with catalogues of any size is small, and diminishing, as is the number of titles most publishers have in print. We may consider several types. First, a very few book publishers have a printed music

34

department, the London houses of Faber and the Oxford University Press being the obvious examples. Not surprisingly, the practices are similar to those that apply in the book trade, Oxford University Press, for example, being one of the very few publishers to allocate an international standard book number to music. Most music publishers set up as specialists, many going back to the eighteenth and nineteenth centuries, and maintain catalogues of international significance. They generally have offices, at least acting as distribution agencies and in some cases publishing their own titles, in countries other than that of origin. In Germany, Bärenreiter, Breitkopf und Härtel, Peters and Schott, in Britain, Boosey and Hawkes, and Novello, are examples; and many have published histories of their houses. Their catalogues include some of the best known composers, who dealt with them, and a smaller quantity of newer work, on a (commercially) more speculative basis.

In recent years, a number of commercial factors have forced many to modify the artistic liberality of earlier days by the business standards of cost accountants; hence the reduced catalogues. One house has reduced from over 10,000 titles to 2,000 in five years. Given the likely size of the market for modern works, many houses find that publishing them for sale is impossible; and instead, they make a small number of copies which they then hire to users. Some specialist libraries and some college libraries deal in hire; but the general public can only obtain such material from the publishers direct. This is the situation with the majority of modern orchestral music, and applies increasingly to chamber music. Inevitably, it means less circulation of the music, fewer performances, formal and informal, and therefore poorer general awareness of the work of new composers in particular. It is fair to add that all concerned are aware of the problem, and some schemes making available hire material in libraries are in operation, and others are being considered. This material is for study, however, not performance.

In general, publishers' hire is geared to the public performance of works, and is therefore onerous on amateur music-making with no performance in mind, a humbler activity

35

perhaps, but a major factor in gaining the awareness referred to. This situation has had the greatest impact on amateur orchestras and chamber groups, whose repertories are therefore restricted, but professional orchestras feel it too. One effect is that frequently enquirers in public libraries have to be told that music is not available for a piece they have heard performed—they assume that if the performance was possible, the music must be available. This is not of course so; not only because of the hire situation, but also because some performing organisations have libraries employing music copyists, and can make their own performing materials, and because some performers make their own editions.

Among the publishing firms, another type of specialist music publisher is the small enterprise, often the creation of a single individual, perhaps the composer himself, using the cheapest possible means of printing to circulate works by composers unable or unwilling to use the larger houses. Such individuals may not cost their time at the commercial rate. In the Eastern bloc, the countries have state publishing houses, the output of which is available through agents in Western countries, although Western experience is generally that of difficulty in obtaining some of this. There is no state run music publisher in the West that I know of; a case could certainly be argued along the lines that, since public money goes, amongst other musical activities, into subsidising concerts which would not otherwise be viable. These are necessary to the artistic health of the population and the availability of materials, from which to perform, contributes to that same end in the face of similar difficulties. Perhaps the appearance of competition with the existing private sector is an obstacle, but with the diminishing size of the latter's activities, there is scope for such enterprise.

Publishers of popular music in sheet form are less in evidence now than formerly, when any new song was released in sheet form—an event roughly comparable with the issue of the record today. Although songs *are* issued in sheet form, the bulk of the material is in albums, many of which, of course, consist of older titles. From the librarian's point of view, it is unfortunate that so many albums partially duplicate one another, and rarely list their contents, although

36

the album is, at least for circulation, much more convenient physically. Although few libraries stock them, sets of parts for dance bands continue to be published, although in much smaller quantity than formerly.

Copyright
The whole subject of copyright in its effects on music is especially vexed, and cannot be considered apart from the economics of publishing. Many members of the music-using public labour under various misconceptions about their rights, and this causes embarrassment when librarians are asked to do things which are illegal. We should distinguish carefully between three closely related areas: the making of copies of printed items, the right to perform a work, and the making of copies of sound recordings (mechanical copyright, dealt with in chapter three). The effect of the law is to forbid the doing of these things without the permission of the copyright holder; and most countries have agreed through international conventions to treat copyright works from other countries as though they were from their own, according them the same protection.

Printed music is, for this purpose, treated on the same basis as books. In practice, one needs to consider the possible rights not only of the composer, but also of authors of verbal text, and editors, where appropriate, as well as the publisher's rights in the graphic image. These last for a period, on the expiry of all of which a work is referred to as non-copyright, or in the public domain. In practice, as this occurs, this means that copying through photocopy machines is legitimate, and that other publishers are free to produce editions of the works—one thinks of Sullivan and Fauré in recent years. Much is talked of the 'fair dealing' clauses in the copyright laws of some countries, which appear to allow some copying for research or private study. In the absence of much case law, the area is notoriously ill-defined, though in Britain a number of parties began (in mid-1978) to discuss a draft agreement circulated by the Music Publishers' Association intended to define it much more closely. The provision of multiple copies for performance of any copyright work, however slight, from photocopier or by hand, is clearly illegal (as well as immoral) for anyone, whether or not part of an educational institution, and music librarians should be warned not to do it. It is the practice of many libraries to make single copies of periodical articles if a declaration is signed, and thus to exchange these copies rather than the original issues. It is widely felt among users that, since the possibility of making cheap copies exists, some form of blanket licensing on behalf of copyright holders would channel the desire which clearly exists into a legal path. In Britain, a government committee under Lord Whitford recommended this in 1977, but it has not yet (mid-1978) happened. Meanwhile, at least one choral society has been successfully prosecuted and heavily fined; which should deal a blow to the 'no-one ever enforces copyright' attitude.

As far as performing right is concerned this is somewhat similar, in that the Performing Rights Society (PRS) in Britain, and the American Society of Composers, Authors and Publishers (ASCAP), and others, will collect fees on behalf of any member composer (in practice, most) and the performer has therefore only to deal with one agency. The practice of music hiring by publishers is related to performing payment; obviously, if a work is only available on hire then a publisher can feel happier that unauthorised performances will not take place without his knowledge. The performance fee may, therefore, be compounded with the hire fee. Again, the amateur, not intending public performance, loses.

Early printed music
Despite the study of bibliography, little was written on the problems of music until the 1950's. Even though some music librarians will not have to deal with pre-twentieth century materials, some of the problems, especially that of ascertaining date of publication, run on into this century. They also underlie many of the problems associated with the musical text of the classics, and sometimes that of composer and title. Most librarians will encounter 'Purcell's Trumpet voluntary' as an alias for Clarke's *Prince of Denmark's march*, from a suite for harpsichord; or the fact that Hoffstetter, not Haydn wrote the 'Haydn opus 3' quartets. The correct attribution in these cases, and many others, is due to the work of bibliography. The study of a piece of music as a physical object

38

involves firstly the answering, as far as possible, of questions: when was it published? What relation does it have to other copies which appear similar? When and why did the changes that may be observed between such copies take place? A lot of this seems like detective work, and may appeal to a similar cast of mind; but its real value lies in what it tells us of the music itself, the composer's intentions, of which any publication is an imprecise record.

The special problems of music bibliography come down to three factors in relation to the date of the events connected with the music: first, very little music carries a date (unlike books); second, the printing of music was mostly from engraved or lithographic plates, from which copies impressed over a long time will have only slight variations; and third, that lack of enforcable copyright at that time led to much piracy, or at least simultaneous and competing issue—for if a composer was, as frequently, inadequately remunerated by one publisher, it is not difficult to see why he tried to get paid by two.

The problems which arise from lack of date, and the consequent need to establish one, are compounded by the different processes used. Bibliographies have established a terminology for the (book) printing processes; and, in using the terms edition, issue, state and impression, they can communicate unambiguously. The application of these terms to music has been the subject of controversy, some people using them in situations which seem analogous; others preferring to avoid them as begging too many questions, and describing as best they can the condition of copies before them. Cataloguers prefer to have a succint and unambiguous way of describing items, and are thus handicapped in dealing with music. Dealers in particular recognise a special magic in the 'first edition'. For one thing, it usually commands a higher price, and this value presumably recognises the close contact which the first edition has with the composer. In many cases, though, the first edition has demonstrably the poorer text.

For those who have not the inclination for this pursuit, or the time to do it justice when an item happens along, the cardinal principle in describing the item, in however brief a catalogue entry, must surely be never to mislead. By all means make an informed guess, if you cannot do better, but make it clear that this is what it is, and if possible note the evidence. Many library catalogues still give a date in all confidence as though it were printed on the title page which is in fact such a guess, and this is to be deplored. Although many libraries never encounter older music, some awareness of the problems can be useful in many situations, and also bears on some of the problems of contemporary publications. A perusal of some of the standard works on bibliography from time to time, particularly if a real problem arises, rather than in the abstract, is therefore to be recommended.

Antiquarian and second hand retailers
A small number of firms specialise in this business, and are well worth getting to know. Some specialise in antiquarian items, early and first editions and such rarities. The librarian whose collections include these will know the sources already. Others sell the more day to day items of a few years ago, and even quite recently, and since music (and indeed books) may go out of print within months of publication, their service is valuable. It has been noticeable that these latter firms have increasingly dealt in new items, while some retailers of new music have increasingly also dealt in second hand material. Such businesses are invariably small, and run by specialists who are knowledgeable beyond what many librarians acquire in their daily business. Most will deal with 'wants' and queries, and almost invariably they publish catalogues, some of which are productions of descriptive bibliography, and are preserved as such after their initial purpose is fulfilled.

The curious and acquisitive librarian will also develop the habit of noticing (and remembering) other sources; secondhand and junk shops occasionally yield items of worth, and auctions of house contents too. Most general dealers feel music somewhat outside their field, and there is an opportunity for building up contacts of use to both sides. A librarian involved in the community will also be offered items by private individuals, and, although tact in letting down gently those who erroneously believe they have items of great value is often called for, so too, worthwhile acquisitions are found.

THREE

RECORDED MUSIC

TO MANY users of the public library music department, the record collection *is* the music library; while some critics of libraries still maintain that they have no business having records at all. The history of record collections seems to shew a similar lack of balance and a desire to take extreme attitudes; and sometimes criteria are applied which we would consider quite untenable elsewhere. The reply to such criticism as that above, which in earlier times often meant a continuing struggle to justify existence at all, was an overreaction. This attitude is noticeable in much of the earlier literature on gramophone record libraries, with an assumption that the new medium had to be defended against the book.

In the context of a music library, a collection of recorded music is surely an essential and integral part of the whole. The basic argument for provision in public libraries is that which applies to books: although individuals can, and most do, acquire collections of their own, these can not attain a size which sustains a growing and wide ranging appreciation of music. Moreover, the realisation of music *in sound* is the heart of the musical experience. Even if the number and range of live music performances was everywhere what it is in the best-provided countries, other factors would prevent it being anything like a regular experience for many. The sound recording is to them an invaluable supplement, along with listening to broadcast music, to a diet which is inevitably restricted in variety, and probably in substance too.

In view of this, one would expect the provision of recordings to be an established part of libraries. In fact, provision has become very uneven. Many academic and conservatory libraries have recognised the force of these arguments;

naturally enough, since their policy-making bodies include people who are mostly well aware of recordings as a part of musical experience. Very few countries have a national archive of sound recordings comparable in size and scope with their national library as a whole. The widest variation is in the standards of provision in public libraries. It is not simply a matter of uneven resources, though this is a major factor. Often, although the policy of collecting records was conceded, the attitude remained that they were a luxury 'extra', and policy in detail has been coloured by this.

The earliest public library record collections were in the USA, the first claimed to be at St Paul's, Minnesota in 1913. By 1940 there were some twenty-five public library loan collections, and several university libraries had records. The national archive (at the Library of Congress Music Division) was well under way. By contrast, in the UK there were two public library collections, and there appears to be no evidence of any records in universities at that time. The British Institute of Recorded Sound was not yet in existence. When it was founded, in 1948, it was not for many years in a position to be in any way comparable with its transatlantic equivalent.

On the continent of Europe, the public record collections as part of libraries largely grew up in the 1950's. Austria and Germany, and later France, had established national archives of recorded sound, supplemented to some extent as elsewhere, perhaps unintentionally, by the archives of the broadcasting organisations. The tradition of commerical record libraries in Europe, particularly in the Netherlands and Scandinavia, made records available before the library net-work had concerned itself with such provision on the present scale. In Britain on the other hand, the number of such commercial libraries in records was always very small (in spite of the strong earlier tradition of 'circulating libraries', ie commercial ones) and has now almost vanished. Coverage in the USA is now extensive, quite small towns having services, and in Britain most authorities now have services, though in all these countries the standards of provision still vary widely.

In all the 'developed' countries, the provision of recorded music in libraries is closely associated with the considerable

growth of the record industry, and with broadcast performance. This has increased public awareness of a wide range of
music, and has to some extent been the result of increased
coverage of music at all levels of education. It is difficult to
guess what effect this has had on live concerts, especially as
regards the range of provision, since in Britain, for example,
this has narrowed in the period, whereas in Germany it has
not. The level of subsidy from the public purse, and the
willingness of the man in the street to spend the sums asked
for concerts, are further variables. There are similarly various
schools of thought on record provision, the two most vexed
being on acquisition policy and on the question of direct
charges.

Within a point of view which has often seen records as an
extravagance in a library, popular music has been equated
with ephemeral music; and some have argued for no provision,
on the basis that it is a dissipation of resources. Against this
it has been said that most libraries have dealt in ephemera to
some extent; lending libraries have some provision for light
romantic fiction, for example. More importantly, it is often
a misconception to equate the various 'popular' music forms
with ephemera. We can see a change in attitude, for example,
to jazz; this would generally have been put in the ephemeral
category twenty years ago, and is now acknowledged to
be a 'serious' form (whatever that means precisely) by
those who are not listeners to it. What then of progressive
rock, rhythm and blues, country and western, to pick a few
examples?

Most public authorities in the countries referred to, and
their enabling legislation, recognise the legitimacy of public
circulating collections of records. However, the provision
varies from that which is free of immediate charge to the
user (the generally accepted standard for books) to that for
which a charge is made, either a 'reasonable charge' which
recovers some of the cost while, it is hoped, preventing no
one who wishes to use the service from doing so; or the
whole cost, which will be a deterrent to many. The policy of
making a charge clearly treats recordings as different from
books; yet for music, the recording is primary, the book
secondary. The record is seen as recreational, the book

43

educational—another of the much discussed divisions in library policy, although for many music is a formal or informal study, and a great number of books are clearly recreational. There is also the difficulty of mixed media. A book may have a cassette enclosed at the end and remain a book, while a cassette has a substantial accompanying booklet yet is a cassette, as far as policy is concerned. This anomaly will become more noticeable as the availability and provision of such packages increase—and they are doing so.

Libraries are rightly encouraged to do what they can to extend their contact with those groups in society who do not naturally turn to them. Much is now done, at considerable (legitimate) expense for various disadvantaged groups. The levying of any charge, however 'reasonable', inevitably narrows the range of people who use the service; and an acquaintance with the clientele of those record libraries, in Britain at any rate, who make a charge, bears this out. Acquisition policy is not so difficult to determine for academic and special libraries; here as elsewhere it is directly related to the needs of the relatively small number of users, as far as these can be determined or predicted. There is, frequently, a reference collection—a feature not often found among public libraries, many of whom have well-established reference libraries (of books). The provision of such a collection will clearly demand equipment for public listening.

The media in which sound recordings are to be stocked will, it is suggested later, largely be a choice between either or both disc and cassette tape in most general libraries, with open-reel tape in some special situations, particularly for longer-term storage. Ideally, tape requires rewinding periodically to avoid transfer of magnetic charges to adjacent positions; though in larger collections this counsel of perfection is impossibly costly in time.

Much selection in libraries of records, or indeed other materials is concerned with taste. It is often suggested, and is valid in choosing recordings, that the librarian should be a little ahead, aware of trends (and that they may be passing fashions) but using the familiar to lead users to less familiar, and thus widen horizons. This places a heavy responsibility, in the need to have wide horizons and catholic taste in the

44

first place. Certain areas of music provoke strong enthusiasm; the librarian should appear (if one dare not say 'be') enthusiastic equally over all areas of the subject, adapting like a chameleon to the enthusiasms of individual patrons.

Record purchasing—supply
A library will, within policy on subject and medium of provision, be faced with a number of difficulties not met with for books. The state of the record industry and of retailing, and the lack of bibliographic control, will be apparent immediately. As with books, one can buy from a local retailer, or a specialist supplier for libraries. The local shop will be geared to supplying public demand, and the range of stock may be somewhat limited; it will be that which is most in demand however, and its convenience as a local source is considerable. Records not in stock, at least those issued by the major companies, can often be ordered. In general, the supply of such items is slow by the standards of booksellers. The major advantages, especially to a small library, of the specialist suppliers, is their greater range of stock and of knowledge, and the availability of servicing. All records will have to be checked visually, if substantial numbers are not to be returned; and most libraries use outer plastic sleeves, along with labels and tickets. These, as well as cataloguing services, are available 'at source' from suppliers, and, as long as they are satisfactory can save a good deal of staff time. There is usually flexibility to meet individual needs and preferences.

—Selection
In the case, now less frequent, of beginning a new record library, the initial stock should be planned on a 'classified' basis, dividing the field into areas and estimating the relative sizes—as is described in a number of sources. One should not hesitate to adjust the proportions to emphasise areas known to be of local relevance; and in countries outside Europe, there is little to be said for the heavy reliance on the European tradition that has, in fact, been seen. This plan can be linked to the coverage of music and books on music, and some kind of plan is useful in later stages if the stock is not to become unbalanced; opera, light orchestral music or rock,

for example, can easily become out of hand if the demands of their particular pressure groups are not kept in perspective. Within these categories, the initial choice is on a basis of musical relevance; and this calls for some experience of the field.

This needs emphasising, since the selection tools are largely comparative, and geared to artists, performances and recording quality, all of which are secondary. The first task, however important these other elements are, is to build a collection of musical works—which term, although implying the highbrow, of course includes all music within the policy guidelines. This course is much to be recommended at the outset, rather than drawing up a list of titles to be acquired (or following a published stock list) since the only way to become reasonably familiar with the field is to break it down into smaller units. Those who are initially daunted had better take the plunge sooner rather than later if they are to have continuing responsibility for stock selection. This approach also allows of co-operation between staff if more than one is involved, as should be the case with a collection of any size.

The process of stock control and development, especially in a circulating library, is one which occupies a heavier proportion of staff time than with books. This is largely due to the relatively short life of a record in library circulation, and of a particular recording in the publisher's catalogue. The turnover is faster, and replacement of the same recording less likely. In this stage of development, it will be easier to consider artists, and to provide several versions of the more popular works, both for the longer term (since no performance is definitive) and to allow for the many users who will expect the library to provide an opportunity for them to compare alternatives before deciding on their own purchases. A problem which is bound to concern the librarian at an early stage is that of bargain labels. How far should the library purchase these in preference to the full-priced discs? Most libraries acquire a proportion of them, but if dependence on them is forced by the budget, the stock as a whole suffers. There are several commercial reasons why items are sold on bargain labels.

If this expression has not been met, it should be explained that pricing of records is determined by the issue of a record on one of the manufacturer's 'labels' each of which has a prefix and often a popular title, the prefix being followed by the record's individual number. All records therefore have a numerical indentification used in ordering, and though the scheme has not quite the consistency of ISBN, it predates it considerably and is universally used for records. A bargain label is one on which the price fixed is substantially below the full price—there is also a 'mid-price' bracket. Bargains are usually re-issues of older recordings, or performances by artists of lesser (commercial) standing. Although usually single records, sets of, for example, all Beethoven's symphonies are encountered. These bargain sets may well have advantages for the library and often are from first-rate artists; the disadvantage for circulation is that they may have to be lent as single discs rather than sets. Other bargains will have to be considered in comparison with alternative higher-priced recordings; it is well to have some overall rule of thumb on the proportion of such issues to be acquired.

New recordings and reviews
In the absence of any satisfactory discographic control, the principal source is a number of periodicals giving details of new releases, some aimed at the general record-buying public, others at librarians. These, along with such information as can be obtained from manufacturers direct, will furnish information on new and forthcoming releases, and will also provide reviews of records. It is an impossible task for the librarian to listen to all prospective purchases, and therefore past experience of the artists and the recording companies, largely supplemented by the opinions of reviewers, will have to suffice.

The librarian familiar with book reviews should be aware that record reviewers in general write for a different audience, and employ different criteria; and this is unfortunate for library use. Just as it was argued that the intrinsic musical value of the pieces should be the basis of the selection, so it should be the first question asked in considering a new recording: does my library need another recording of this piece? While book reviews do largely refer to the content, most record reviews compare new releases with existing ones of the work (the first-time recording of a piece being a

47

relatively rare event) in terms of performance and recording quality. If a recording is unique and the work should be represented, there is no selection problem. Now much of the comparison between recordings is susceptible to the pressure of commerce, especially marketing. Records are often issued because there is some short-term topicality, or a boom in some artist or composer is built up. The music librarian, while facing an increased demand due to these effects, must maintain a balance from a longer term, international view; one remembers exaggerated interest in Sibelius, Vaughan Williams, Mahler which must have left many libraries overstocked when things settled down.

Reviews

The regular listing of records commercially available in Britain is the quarterly *Gramophone classical catalogue*, with popular catalogues by artist and title also quarterly, and an annual *Spoken word and miscellaneous catalogue*. This is most successful for standard repertory classical items and current pop numbers issued by the larger established companies. There is a considerable grey area of material, which falls between the classical and pop categories, which is difficult to trace if listed; and many of the products on smaller labels do not figure at all. In the USA the *Schwann* catalogues list classical records monthly, and most other categories in the semi-annual *Schwann-2*. New releases are listed in several periodicals which also review at least a proportion of them; in Britain the *Gramophone, Hi-fi news* (which incorporates the old *Audio and record review*), *Records and recording* among the magazines and the *EMG monthly letter*. In the USA *American record guide, Stereo review* and *High fidelity* are primary sources.

The *Gramophone* (1923-   ) is largely a source of reviews, with some other text, by a panel of distinguished names in the field, each with specialist interest. Earlier recordings of the same work are compared. The catalogues referred to above give the issue in which each record was reviewed, enabling the review to be traced quickly. Some jazz and popular items are included, but the main interest is in the classical repertory.

Hi-fi news has fewer and shorter reviews, but devotes a good deal of space to articles on technical matters and the industry, and has occasional articles on special topics. It has sections devoted to new rock, jazz, light music and folk music.

Records and recording has a more 'popular' style, and besides reviews includes information, largely on 'personalities', especially artists.

All these three cover cassettes and discs. Records only are covered in *The EMG monthly letter*, EMG hand-made gramophones, London, which contains solely reviews, very short and pithy, and titles from which are collected into the annual *The art of record buying*. Although a trade publication, the reviews are as objective as one could reasonably expect, and well regarded. A 'rating' system is used in the annual.

In the USA *American record guide* has, besides reviews of home and some imported records, articles on music (especially composers) and events in recording. *High fidelity*, besides reviews, covers the technical side, reviewing equipment and also runs articles on musical aspects.

Stereo review (formerly *Hi-fi/stereo review*) is again wider than just reviews, of which these three give fair coverage. Jazz records are reviewed in *Jazz journal international*, which circulates in both the UK and North America, and in *Black music and jazz review*, similarly international which covers new recordings in soul and reggae as well as jazz. Rock and pop are covered by *New musical express* and *Melody maker* in London, and *Billboard* in the USA, from a more directly commercial view. The UK and US charts are included in *Black music*, and the specific charts in the others.

Specialist sources in Europe include at least one major periodical from most countries, which can be traced as necessary; the English speaking user can probably gain information in spite of language problems from the French *Disques*, the Italian *Musica e dischi* and the German *Fono Forum* and *Musica*. In addition, the reviews and lists in library periodicals, especially *Notes,* are a major source, and many general interest periodicals carry record reviews; though the law of diminishing returns operates against too wide a proliferation of titles for regular inspection.

In using reviews one tries to see some critics' work often enough to gain some idea of their own prejudices in a

49

subjective field, without coming to follow any individuals too closely. A regular following of three or four sources is better than infrequent dipping into much more. Finally, although comprehensive listening is not possible, some listening, formulating one's own views, followed by comparison of these with those of the reviewers, is very salutary. Radio programmes devoted to new recordings are a great convenience and well worth following. Record libraries are particularly prone to follow current availability and trends at the expense of the archival value of material, which is considerable for recordings. Some works of merit are not always available, or may only be available if imported. There is more reluctance to consider foreign records for purchase than foreign books, simply because of the difficulties posed. Sometimes a deletion in one country remains available elsewhere. It will be necessary to use a specialist for such recordings, direct purchase from abroad being a last resort, and the supply situation varies so much from country to country as to make general advice worthless, but the librarian is urged to consider how far such sources are tapped.

The need to keep some recordings aside for reference use has taken a second place to that of running a circulating collection, at least in public libraries. Clearly a circulating collection, with its relatively fast turnover of stock, will fill the reference function much less efficiently than a lending library of books will support reference enquiries. Putting aside some recordings, even informally, is desirable even in medium-sized collections, and larger ones should have a formalised acquisition of such material. A pattern for a scheme of co-operation on, amongst other objectives, the preservation of such material as has lasting value among a number of library authorities has been set by the Greater London Audio specialisation scheme, GLASS, in which the thirty-two boroughs divide the area between them.

Apart from the need to preserve some material, any circulating library will have to discard stock regularly and systematically, and usually because it is worn out. Such recordings must be withdrawn immediately; the harm done once users find a lowering in these standards is considerable. A smaller number of records, though not worn, may prove to go out on loan so infrequently that their retention cannot be justified. The temptation to retain such dead wood should be resisted, and the principle accepted that a proportion of the budget must be set aside for new purchases to fill the gaps thus left.

Forms of recordings

Any librarian handling recordings will be aware of the need to be familiar with the problems of records and tapes, and the equipment needed to play them; and, indeed, many of the books and training courses on the subject will go into greater detail than is possible here. Library students have traditionally studied the history and manufacture of the book, even if much of the knowledge is rarely put to the test thereafter. In dealing with recorded materials, however, the problems are met daily both in using the equipment oneself, and in dealing with the public who expect to be able to obtain advice. Much of the relationship with record users turns on the attitude we can instil in them by example, as well as precept and knowledge.

Of the various means of recording and transmitting sound, the librarian will encounter the LP record, tape, particularly cassette tape, and the radio, much more frequently than any other—at least in the foreseeable future. The original shellac disc running at 78 rpm ,is, for all but the most specialist archival purposes, superseded; its fragility and rapid rate of wear being too great a disadvantage in a library. Many recordings of lasting interest have been transferred to LP, a more convenient arrangement than transfer to plastic discs in the 78 rpm large groove format, which therefore require special equipment. Similarly, the mono disc is virtually superseded, surviving only in these transfers to LP of earlier recordings, and should not be purchased in any case where the stereo alternative exists. Libraries should themselves use, and require of their users, equipment designed for use with stereo records. As far as quadraphonics is concerned, it is perhaps still early to generalise; but it now seems very unlikely to sweep the field in the way stereo did, ousting the earlier form.

Tape formats raise more problems. Open reel tape is still used widely for recording, but pre-recorded tapes are very much less in evidence since the cassette was introduced. There is also some variety in speed and format of open reel, and it is not a practicable alternative for circulating collections, though larger libraries may need equipment for its use. At the highest end of the market, it is at the time of writing the reliable format for making the highest quality of recording in the hands of an operator of some experience, and is so used in most professional recording situations. Cassette, on the other hand, has a large and expanding quantity of pre-recorded material—but not yet matching disc—and can be used for making recordings which, especially with Dolby noise reduction, are acceptable in quality for most purposes. It is much easier to use, and more convenient. If the standards of reliability of the motor mechanisms in particular are not yet up to the best of disc or open-reel tape, they are improving. The other tape package, the cartridge (8-track), is intrinsically less satisfactory mechanically; and, apart from use in cars in the USA, where legislation prohibits cassette, and for continuous background music in hotels, supermarkets and the like, it is rapidly falling from favour. It cannot be recommended for the library.

In practice, therefore, we have the LP disc and the cassette; and many libraries are having to deal in both, duplicating subject matter for the sake of the medium. Cassette has some advantages: it is less susceptible to accidental damage, it may be played on poor equipment while thereafter being satisfactory for the best equipment, and the small physical size is convenient. It is very useful where repeated starting and stopping within an item is to take place. Disc has a larger quantity of material available (this may not always be so) and is, by virtue of its large size, less of a security risk. It provides better quality at the cost of the best equipment, and the existing record collector who has good equipment, well maintained, which has cost a good deal of money is not willingly going to change it.

Record care
The ideal conditions for storage were described in a classic report by Pickett and Lemcoe for the Library of Congress in

1959 (*see* reading list) and, in spite of changing fashions, their conclusions have not been seriously challenged. In library practice, this means as recommendations, storage vertically in small groups between partitions, preferably under light pressure, in controlled temperature and humidity, in flat inner wrappers inside the outer sleeve—almost invariably nowadays of polythene, the cheaper paper wrappers of some companies being replaced. In play, a dust-removing device is desirable, records should be played individually and placed on the turntable by hand, the arm being lowered gently either by hand or mechanically onto the lead-in groove.

Circulating libraries will wish to display records to best advantage, and this means taking some liberty with the first point; the browser box with slightly raked dividers has become virtually universal for such collections. Most libraries protect the sleeve with a further clear plastic jacket, which may bear the necessary stationery for issue purposes. A reference in a top corner aids filing, since the layout of a sleeve is much less consistent than a book spine.

Users are encouraged to care for records as much by the attitude of the staff as by instruction, but leaflets and posters summarising the points most likely to be overlooked are widely used. Checks of record condition on return are practised in most libraries, and damage charged for. It is quite usual to check styli of new members on joining, and regularly thereafter. For this a microscope, of at 100x magnification (ideally binocular) with a strong source of illumination is necessary. Experience shews that many users regard styli as everlasting: the most expensive diamond styli are certainly not. One manufacturer claims some two thousand sides life under good conditions, and for sapphires very much less. In fact sapphires, although apparently cheaper, are not so for a given life, and are an extra hazard, not to be recommended. The fact that a stylus is new is no guarantee: increasingly a proportion of brand new styli are discovered to have flaws sufficient to damage a record, and new styli should therefore be inspected like any other.

Many users are aware of the possible damage from a stylus, or even an unsatisfactory pick-up arm; much fewer realise that motor and turntable faults can cause damage. Hum and rumble, transmitted to the arm by inadequate mountings of motor, table and arm, can make the pick-up distort the grooves of a disc, as can the vibrations caused by wear on the cheaper drive mechanisms. The recommendation must be that equipment should be checked regularly—both the libraries' and the users'. The latter find this difficult to assimilate; having paid a good deal for their equipment they often expect it to last for ever. The analogy with a car, where servicing reduces wear and damage, may be helpful.

The cleaning of records may, on the library's scale, be sufficient of a problem to justify the acquisition of a cleaning machine; ideally, records should not be allowed to get so dirty, a dust remover and anti-static device being sufficient. But any larger collection will find this problem arising frequently enough to justify such a machine, as well of course as hand cleaning. The other warning which needs regular reinforcement is that on the effects of even quite gentle heat: a sunny day in a library will see the return of several fatalities from inside cars, behind windows and so on. The display of some outstanding casualties can be salutary.

Cassette care
The cassette is very much less susceptible to damage of the kind just described. Occasionally, a motor may take up sufficiently roughly to tear tape from time to time. The longer playing cassettes use the thinnest tape, and are perhaps better avoided. There is of course a difficulty about erasure; it should normally not be possible accidentally to over-record a pre-recorded tape, a mechanical means of disabling the erase head being used. Some users discover how to render this inoperative, and such malicious damage will probably go unnoticed until the next loan. The quality available from this medium has improved substantially in the decade or so of availability, and the Dolby noise reduction system has reduced the hiss inherent in tape. Developments, both technical and commercial may be expected and will doubtless be featured in the periodicals.

Copyright
The wide distribution of tape recorders, making easily possible the copying of recordings, makes a caution necessary at

this point. Both the copying, for whatever purpose, and the public performance of commercial recordings are, under copyright law of most countries 'restricted acts'. Performance, such as recitals, may be permitted on the copyright holders' behalf by one of the licensing organisations (on payment of a fee) in the USA and UK; but there is no equivalent in record copying of the 'fair dealing' concept which has grown up in copying documents. The only safe course for a library is not to permit or condone copying unless permission has been granted. It may be noted that in West Germany a licensing arrangement is paid for by a tax on recorders and tapes, so that the purchaser may, within limits, make copies. A recent report in Britain has recommended such a system, but it is not yet implemented. It must be highly desirable that some practicable means of regularising a situation, where now the law is widely broken, should be achieved.

Recordings—classification and cataloguing
It is very desirable in the case of recordings of music to treat material as far as possible on the same basis as the printed versions of the same items. Clearly recordings will be accommodated separately, and in some cases the catalogue may be separate; public collections generally have separate catalogues, academic and college libraries often preferring what may seem more logical, a catalogue in which all versions of an item are brought together irrespective of the medium of presentation. Much of the argument about general principles of arrangement and cataloguing, to be discussed in chapter six, applies to recordings. However, we should note some particular difficulties.

The arrangement of records where display and browsing is not of importance is most easily done by record manufacturers' numbers, which seems much easier than by accession number. Most circulating collections, however, require browsing, and hence some classified order is generally preferred. The browser box is greatly preferred by users to shelving, book fashion, as is testified by a number of libraries who have made the change. Composer order is very rare, as indeed with printed music, but opinions differ as to the kind of classification which is useful. In some circumstances detailed classification is preferred, but most prefer a small number of broad subject groups: opera, concertos, jazz and so on, within which order is, theoretically at least, by composer or call number. The rapid turnover of such stock, however, tends to make the order unreliable unless regularly checked, but borrowers seem to accept a degree of disorder within categories. A code for such groupings, perhaps expanded into a Cutter number, can be placed on a top corner of the sleeve for ease of filing. Public library collections in most countries now employ open access with some scheme along these lines; libraries in colleges and universities tend not to regard browsing as a necessity, and prefer book-style shelving and a simpler order.

Cassettes raise quite different problems, not least of security, and open-access is less often used. Either boxes only are displayed, or a closed-access system is used. Various racks and stands have been designed to lock a number of cassettes which remain visible; opening the mechanism is a problem in a library of any size. A satisfactory system allowing open access, which is clearly as desirable as with discs, without serious security risk, is yet to be devised and a compromise will have to be adopted.

It is noticeable, both in public libraries and in college and university libraries, that a high proportion of enquiries for recordings are those where composer and title are quoted. It may be surprising then that composer order filing has not been used more frequently; but a serious problem is the number of recordings containing more than one work, and often by more than one composer. The main catalogue will have to cope with this problem. Whether added entries or analytical entries are used, a number greater than is usual in book cataloguing will have to be employed if some short pieces are to have entries at all; since there are pieces which almost always figure in anthologies, or in the jargon of the industry, as 'fillers',—short items used to fill the remaining space on a disc when a substantial work takes the majority.

A major decision as to the level of cataloguing necessary should be taken in the light of knowledge of the questions it will be needed to answer. For many collections serving a largely entertainment need (and others) much detailed disco-graphic information is redundant. Composer, title in some systemised form, and tracing information, are primary; along with a note as to performance. Larger libraries will prefer a full entry, along the same lines as the book catalogue. Smaller libraries may find it more economical to purchase catalogue information, in card (or machine-readable) form, and some suppliers offer this service.

For some music the performer acquires the equivalent status of a composer, especially in jazz and folk music. The name of the performer should *in such cases* be used as heading. This should not be extended to other performers, best dealt with in a performer index, since the inter-filing of added entries under performer in a catalogue is a source of confusion.

Recordings: community involvement

It is surprising in view of the widespread acceptance of the recording in libraries and of a library's duty toward local material, that more libraries do not make recordings, even of modest technical standard. Local events, especially but not only of music could be recorded, in the same way that, for example, collections of slides of local views are built up in some libraries. The broadcasts of local radio stations are also an obvious source, provided the necessary permission can be obtained.

Many libraries, however, use recordings as a source of recitals given to publicise the collection, and specific aspects of it in relation to other events in the community. The plan-ning of a collection of recordings in a library should take into account the need to provide suitable accommodation and equipment for such work; and it might be borne in mind that provision for live music-making, under library sponsorship, does not involve much more expenditure if the first is accepted. The goodwill, as well as the increased use of the library's materials, which arises from this kind of provision is considerable.

FOUR

LITERATURE OF MUSIC: BOOKS

LIBRARIANS will feel happier in dealing with the literature of music where the form is familiar, and bibliographic and other reference works cover the subject as well as most; although there are relationships with other disciplines, philosophy and religion, literature and physics in particular, the subject is also fairly selfcontained and distinct. Librarians unused to music should bear in mind that books are a secondary source in the field, and the collection of music literature will be intimately related to the primary sources in the library, and as far as the physical constraints allow, the closeness of the relationship will be emphasised. Thus, although the basic layout may separate material, there is much scope for ingenuity in the provision of special displays which emphasise the interdependence.

This chapter will briefly consider the various categories of writing about music, with a number of general observations. The reader is encouraged to examine the works themselves as widely as possible, and a number of examples are quoted in order to assist the process. The lifetime task of examining, judging and noting an ever larger quantity of material is only possible if individual items can be fitted into some frame of reference. The examples chosen will largely be in English, but the English speaking music libarian is well advised to cultivate some French, German and Italian at least. A knowledge of languages is, of course, an advantage; but the librarian who lacks it should not be daunted from tackling foreign language items, and with increasing experience much information can be extracted from foreign reference works when command of the language is limited. A set of multilingual dictionaries is indispensible, and a work such as

George von Ostermann's *Manual of foreign languages* New York, Central Books Co 1952, is very useful in giving an outline of syntax and habits of expression.

Two general guides to the literature of music should be to hand in almost every music library, and familiar to any serious student. Vincent Duckles's *Music reference and research materials* New York, Free Press 1974; London, Collier-Macmillan, is the third edition of a most comprehensive list of nearly two thousand works, arranged in categories, with critical annotation. Few music librarians would claim to have seen more than a proportion of them, but the work is the easiest way to check and compare what exists, and to find details of any specific work, when necessarily much of what is contained will not be to hand. One can only hope it will continue to be re-edited from time to time.

Sadly this is not possible for John Davies's *Musicalia* Pergamon 1969—the second edition of a book which drew heavily on its author's articles in *Library world*. Unlike Duckles's work, it can (and should) be read as well as consulted. It is an intensely practical work with a good many observations incorporated into a discussion of the literature as it is approached by various kinds of music user. An indication of the style of presentation employed in some of the works discussed is given by the incorporation of pages of facsimile in the text.

A third work which, a few years ago, would have been placed unhesitatingly in the same rank as these two is R D Darrell's *Schirmer's guide to music and musicians* New York, Schirmer 1951. This employed the dictionary sequence of names and subjects characteristic of library catalogues in the USA, and had a bias to the popular rather than the academic approach, including many not generally regarded as reference books, which usefully complemented other works. It can still be used, with some caution, in many aspects of the field.

Many other such general surveys will be encountered in libraries, and the choice of a more experienced librarian, especially in the selection of those items which acquire the premium shelf space within reach from the desk, can often be noticed, overtly or surreptitiously. The relevant sections of the more general guides, especially A J Walford's *Guide to reference material*, 3rd ed, Library Association, vol 3; and Constance Winchell's *Guide to reference books*, 8th ed, American Library Association, 1967, are also worthy of examination. These works then, are of a kind that repay being constantly to hand. The kinds of writing about music will now be examined.

Music history—general 'classical'
The core of any collection of books about music is what is broadly referred to as history. The earliest writings in the genre, the histories of Burney and of Hawkins, which both date from 1776, strike us as being as much about the writers as representative of the taste of the time, as about their subject. It is usual today to expect a more detached approach, even when attempting evaluation. The large multivolume histories in series such as the *New Oxford history of music* or its predecessor, and the *Pelican history of music*, or the works issued by Norton/Dent and Prentice-Hall have the advantage that specialists in the various periods can be called upon, even if this means some variety of approach and presentation. A different sort of variety, as well as a shorter treatment, can be observed in the single volume comprehensive history, although in the hands of authors like P H Lang, D J Grout or A Einstein, a unity of view is strongly felt. Harman and Mellers achieved the compromise of a work issued both in single and multivolume form. Most of these books stress the social and cultural influences of music and acting upon it. A more popular category of history is the illustrated work. Two French writers, both translated into English, are M Pincherle and J Chailley, and although bias in some of their judgments is evident, they cover their fields in an attractive and popular style. In a single work some errors of fact are more likely, since no one scholar will be as expert in all fields as the specialist, but the sense of continuity and build-up is evident. Clearly some representation of both forms will be provided in most general libraries. It is necessary to put a number of accounts of music together before a reader begins to acquire a rounded picture, and such works are complementary. Most formal

61

courses of training in music require the reading of such works to provide an overall frame of reference before embarking on a more detailed consideration of individual times and places.

Some idea of the problems and scope of music history, and of the criteria by which works may be judged, can be gained from Sir Jack Westrup's small volume *An introduction to musical history*, Hutchinson 1955, and in particular the first two chapters. This and a companion volume, Thurston Dart's *The interpretation of music*, 1954, which discusses the relation between musical sources and performance will give much information which will help the librarian to understand the needs and problems of the musicians he meets.

Many books deal with particular aspects of music history, the music of some time or place, or in a style. Often the scope is limited enough to allow for a writer with considerable mastery of detail and of the overall picture, and in some cases to be a known authority on the subject. Even then the subject will often break down to individual composers, and in the best of such works the difference between a compilation approach, such as Gerald Abraham's *Slavonic and romantic music* Faber 1968 or a work written as a whole like Martin Cooper's *French music from the death of Berlioz to the death of Fauré* Oxford University Press 1970 is not noticed, each painting an integrated picture of its topic. Some others in this genre are little more than a collection of potted biographies, and this may not be apparent from the title. Much of the information contained may duplicate other works in such cases.

—African and Asian music
Different libraries will come to their own view of the value of such specialist studies as cover the music of cultures far removed from their own. There has been a considerable widening of popular taste in such matters, and in the attention they receive in the study of music history at all levels. This is reflected in the output of works on music of African and Asian traditions for example. A European library will still, and rightly, have a substantial coverage of its own tradition; but other cultures should be represented. There are now many more works giving an outline coverage of these fields.

Folk music

A somewhat similar widening of libraries' coverage, in folk music traditions, or in academic contexts, in ethnomusicology, has again followed a widening of popular interest. While of course covering the field generally, if in no great depth, there is a particular responsibility to deal with any local traditions, both in sources and writing. Books dealing with the methods of folk music conservation are not yet numerous; the reader might look at Cecil Sharp's *English folk song: some conclusions*, 1907 reprinted Wakefield, E P Publishing, 1972 and Maud Karpeles's *An introduction to English folk song* reprinted Oxford University Press, 1973. Since the movement was largely begun in England the bias may here be forgiven; Kodaly's *Folk music of Hungary* Barrie and Jenkins 1971 might widen the view. This is an area which produces great enthusiasts, and a librarian may learn a lot from them, while trying to form a balanced view.

Jazz and pop

This is also especially true of jazz and pop. One has, fortunately, no longer to apologise for these cultures being represented in libraries, at least in books on the subject; although the primary sources of music, printed and recorded, often fare worse. These are both largely documented areas, and a specialist music librarian may be forgiven, in the present state of music education, for a lack of knowledge here relative to other fields. A lack of enthusiasm is forgiveable only if it is not apparent from the selection of books; the opposite pitfall of allowing specific enthusiasms to run away with the stock is also to be watched. Those who wish to widen their horizons might start, for jazz, with either Leroy Ostransky's *Understanding jazz* Englewood Cliffs, NJ, Prentice-Hall, 1977, or Marshall Stearns' *The story of jazz* London, New York, OUP, 1970, both of which have bibliographies and the latter a list of recordings illustrating the whole tradition; while a more comprehensive coverage including technical detail is given in Mark C Gridley's more recent *Jazz styles* Englewood Cliffs, NJ, Prentice-Hall, 1978, with a bibliography and glossary and a discography which is a useful reference source. Out of an even wider field of writings attempting an introduction to pop, an initial approach via Charlie Gillett *The sound of the city* Sphere, 1971 will find accurate and detailed fact, coupled with a balanced judgement not unduly curbed by considerable enthusiasm. He has also edited *Rock file* 1 to 5, of which number 3, with a list of recordings, is particularly valuable; but all are stimulating, going into more detail in the topics covered. Another general introduction is Nik Cohn's *WopBopaLooBopaLopBamBoom* Paladin, 1970.

Books on musicians—composers
Perhaps the largest single section in any collection of books on music is that devoted to individual musicians. To call such works biographies is perhaps misleading, for many discuss the compositions at least as much, if not more than, the mere facts of the life. Studies of composers can be seen as scholarly, popular or eulogistic with the best achieving something of all three. Those written during or immediately after the lifetime of the subject may have the benefit of the writer's first hand knowledge, but the objectivity of a later study is difficult to achieve. Some composers are well catered for, others of apparently similar standing much less so. Where choice has to be made, the varying intents of the writers will be considered, as will their standing and previous work; but, in any case, most of these books will be well covered by reviews. There are in the field one or two series of publications, and a decision in these cases will probably be for the series as a whole. The *Master musicians* of Dent, for example, is a well balanced series of some forty titles covering most of the best known composers, *Oxford studies of composers* have tended to go in for less obvious figures, and are slighter volumes. Faber's *Great composers* is a good example of a series well suited to a younger reader but still readable by adults. More specialist are the *BBC music guides,* which deal with a particular genre in the output of a composer each, aimed especially at the listener, who is also catered for by the *Concertgoers companions* of Bingley. The latter contain bibliographies and discographies of the composer, and are useful as works of reference for the librarian, as well as sources of deeper pleasure while concert

64

going. Two other categories of books on composers are the symposium, where the overview may be sacrificed somewhat in favour of the most authoritative treatment of individual aspects. This approach can be seen in *The Mozart companion*, edited by H C Robbins Landon and Donald Mitchell, Faber 1965, or the series published by Oxford University Press of which such works as *Handel: a symposium* edited by Gerald Abraham, 1954, and *Schumann: a symposium*, 1952, with the same editor, are particularly distinctive contributions to the literature on their subjects, containing fact and judgment not available elsewhere; as are those on Schumann, Liszt and Chopin edited by Alan Walker and published by Barrie and Jenkins.

Many composers' letters have been published, and are obvious source material for the serious student. In some cases, along with careful editing and some text, they can be read with pleasure by others: Percy Young's *The letters of Edward Elgar* Bles 1956, illustrates this type. This approach has been extended to cover a wide range of contemporary source material, much not easily available elsewhere, in a readable form with continuous text in *The Bach reader*, edited by Hans T David and Arthur Mendel Dent, 1966.

At the most subjective end of the scale are the auto-biographies or memoirs—some of which are valuable contributions, not only to a study of their writers, but of a wider view of their milieu. Berlioz, Rimsky-Korsakov and Stravinsky (the last in the form of conversations with Robert Craft) have left highly personal accounts whose continuing availability testify to their popular as well as scholarly appeal.

Performers
Turning from composers to performers, there is a marked shift of emphasis. The majority of books are written about contemporary figures, and shew the spirit of popular adulation which has and still does extend much more readily to the performer. This is not to say that there are not balanced views of the place of a given performer in their musical society, but each work will need more care in examination. The author is less likely to be someone of known standing, and the ghosted autobiography may well be part of the

artist's publicity machine. Such works are generally well in demand in public libraries, and it is a matter of resources available how far this may be satisfied. A small number of books on performers are contributions to the study of performance practice or instrumental technique. Writers on performers from 'pop' are unlikely to attempt the standards of criticism used elsewhere, and few of their readers would appreciate it if they did. Unfortunately for the librarian, there is much duplication in the field of glossy illustrated biography of pop stars, and little to choose between them. Public circulating collections will need a representative selection, but in reference work, information from such items should be cross checked if possible.

Style and analysis
A small number of works have discussed some aspect of composition or style in some technical detail. Such works will assume a knowledge both of some historical background and of the rudiments of musical grammar. The Viennese classical style is discussed by Charles Rosen in *The classical style* Faber 1971, and the 'Second Viennese school' in Josef Rufer's *Composition with twelve notes* Berlin, Hesses verlag 1952, and in English translation Barrie and Rockcliffe 1954; New York, Macmillan. Two books which brought in what were new approaches to the analysis of music and have had a considerable influence are Rodolph Reti's *The thematic process in music*, Faber 1961 and Deryck Cooke's *The language of music* Oxford University Press 1959. All these works approach music by way of analysis, describing in various ways what has been written and comparing and explaining the relationships of parts to the whole.

The expression 'musical analysis' will most readily bring to mind a more limited approach to specific works, giving some detail of the internal structure of the music and of any external information which bears on it. These are consulted by many music lovers before concert going, as well as by those required to study a piece in detail during some course. Donald Tovey's six volumes of *Essays in musical analysis*, Oxford University Press 1935-44, written originally as programme notes, seem likely to survive although more than half a century old, and a few of the works described have departed the repertory. Anthony Hopkins has turned the style of his successful radio talks into book form in *Talking about music* Pan, 1977.

A few authors provide analysis specifically related to the needs of certain examination syllabuses. Annie Warburton's *Analyses of musical classics* Longman 1963-71, in three volumes, mostly reprinted articles from *Music teacher*, is an example. Concertgoers in particular will also be interested in criticism of performance; from the historical fascination of Hanslick or George Bernard Shaw (writing as *Corno di Bassetto*) describing the concert scene of Vienna in the last century or London in the nineties, and touching many other questions too, to contemporary writings.

Music theory
Under this somewhat dated expression it is convenient to group the books dealing with the rudiments and 'grammar' of music—the categories of study which are traditional for more advanced work leading to composition: harmony, counterpoint, form and orchestration—as well as some literature of acoustics, where, in a general library the music and physics section will meet.

The study of the basics of musical grammar has changed in a way not unlike that of the grammar of language. Older books will appear somewhat heavy in style, and will express their guidance in the form of rules. The modern student is given a lighter presentation, where principles are derived from a study of the most admired practitioners. This approach is characteristic of Imogen Holst's *An ABC of music* Oxford University Press 1963, and Otto Karolyi's *Introducing music* Penguin 1965, and such works can safely be offered to adults, where many introductions aim at children. The older aproach can be observed in the writings of Ebenezer Prout, the high priest of the method, and many writers between his time and the 1960's.

Contact with any schools or colleges in the area of the library will shew which of the courses of harmony are followed, and a selection can be obtained for the general library. While the college library may be required to provide such works in sufficient quantity to support the classes, a public library should not attempt to do so; and requests for extensions to the normal period of loan should be scrutinised with care. It should be explained that, in the parlance of music education, 'harmony' often means the style associated with the chorales of J S Bach and 'counterpoint', the style of Palestrina and Lassus; and while the approach is well understood by those involved, a general reader will often need something discussing a wider set of models. 'Orchestration' is usually referred to scoring for the classical symphony orchestra, with some study of its constituent instruments; but the librarian should not overlook works on scoring or instrumentation for other groups of instruments and styles. Wind and percussion bands and string groups have been catered for, especially by American authors, filling a need created by the popularity of such groups there, and various forms of light music, particularly the dance band, have a distinctive style of instrumental texture which has been written about.

Music has been referred to its fundamentals as a physical phenomenon in a class of works of which Sir James Jeans's *Science and music* Cambridge University Press 1937, reprinted by Dover in 1969, and Alexander Wood's *The physics of music* Methuen 1944, reprinted by Chapman and Hall 1976, are still models. More recent examples sometimes illustrate their argument with an accompanying record, the value of which should override the reluctance some librarians feel at the problems created. An associated subject is musical aesthetics and psychology; here again two early classics remain widely used an influenced much later writing: C E Seashore's *The psychology of music* McGraw Hill 1938, reprinted by Dover in 1968, and Percy Buck's *Psychology for musicians* Oxford University Press 1944. Aesthetics as a branch of philosophy is the subject of parts of a number of courses in education, and the application to music can be seen in a work such as R G Collingwood's *The principles of art* Oxford University Press 1938, which does not refer specifically to music but deals in the general principles against which the comments of, for example, Beethoven and Stravinsky may be set in perspective.

Music teaching

The psychology of music is also regarded as a part of the study of music education. Besides works on the teaching of specific vocal and instrumental techniques, which we may consider with other books on instruments and voices, there are a number of books on the general principles of music education, and many on its practice in specific situations: for example, various grades of school, further education, pre-school children. These will need to be related to the particular educational system practised in the country of the library; and again, some contact with the practitioners is worth a good deal of reading. Three other aspects written about are school opera, about which detailed guidance can be found; the 'music and movement' method of instilling rhythmic appreciation, particularly associated with the name of Ann Driver; and what to many teachers is the problem of assimilating the 'pop' world, which will be many pupils' main musical experience, into a wider understanding. Some specific educational theories and practices are outlined: the Japanese Suzuki method, for example, has several books devoted to it.

Musical instruments

A major section of the available music literature is devoted to works on instruments. The widest coverage, not unnaturally, is on the instruments of the symphony orchestra. There are detailed surveys of the history of instruments, describing their evolution and enabling the reader to see what the form of the instrument in, say, Beethoven's day was like. Anthony Baines's *Woodwind instruments and their history* Faber 1968, *Brass instruments* Faber 1976, and *Musical instruments through the ages* Penguin 1963, are excellent starting points. Benn has a series devoted to the history and modern form of instruments dealt with in a volume each, and the librarian as well as the performer will appreciate the lists of music for the instrument, solo and in ensemble, which are given at the end of each work. The Oxford University Press has a series of smaller works on the modern form of wind, brass and percussion instruments called *Flute technique, Clarinet technique*, and so on, which are reasonably priced and likely to be in the hands of those who study the instruments, but are nonetheless worth having as a set in any library catering for performers. They, too, have lists of music, and the two series together will cover the bibliography of instrumental music for many purposes.

Some works on the technique of instrumental performance border closely on the method, employing a music size format. The publisher Summy-Birchard of Evanston, Illinois, for example, has a series for wind instruments, using titles such as *The art of flute playing*; and in England, Oxford University Press has put out a similar work on the oboe by Evelyn Rothwell, *The oboist's companion*, in three volumes— although there is no sign of any other instrument being thus treated. Surprisingly few of the books on instruments include illustrations in the form of sound recordings, as does Horace Fitzpatrick's *The horn and horn playing* Oxford University Press 1970. There are a few books giving detailed guidance on the repair and maintenance of instruments, and even on their construction. The instrument most frequently 'home-made' is probably the guitar, and do-it-yourself manuals are available.

This is also true of the organ, and with a revival of interest in earlier methods, some old books are enjoying a new lease of life in reprint. One may distinguish three kinds of organist and instrument: the church organist, almost certainly pro-pipes and anti-electronics, but sharply subdivided into the baroque classical and the romantic schools; the cinema organist, which in England at any rate commands an increased following in proportion to its decreased use, like the steam locomotive; and the electronic 'home entertainment' organ, both in commercial and do-it-yourself form. All have their literature (the music, too, is different in each case) and should be catered for to some extent, though the major classifications will lump them together.

The piano has, not surprisingly, a very large quantity of writing on performance and repertoire; and there is material for young and old beginners, and a variety of attainment thereafter. Many teachers will consciously follow the theories of, say, a Matthay or a Schnabel; and for some a single piano composer, Chopin, Liszt or Debussy, perhaps, will be their sole study—all these are catered for. The field is surveyed in Joseph Rezits and Gerald Deatsman's *The pianists resource guide* Park Ridge, Illinois, Pallma Music Corporation 1978, which covers both writings on the piano and music for it; and the librarian may refer to this when unable to place a piano work, as one of the several guides to piano music and its styles.

On the maintenance and tuning of the piano, A H Howe's *Scientific piano tuning and servicing* Clifton, New Jersey, American Piano Supply Company 1963, is a modern standard work; and an exceptionally well illustrated new work is Arthur Reblitz's *Piano servicing, tuning and rebuilding* New York, Vestal Press 1976, for the very serious amateur or professional. The amateur has two new books: Michael Johnson and Robin Mackworth-Young's *Tune and repair your own piano* London, New York, Harcourt Brace Jovanovich 1978, and the well illustrated *Pianos in practice: an owners manual* London, Scholar Press 1978, by Eric Smith.

With the rise in interest in earlier instruments, those keyboard instruments considered obsolescent now have a following and a literature; apart from the harpsichord, the clavichord and spinet are catered for. Here the performer is probably obliged to maintain the instrument, and this is recognised. In the case of such wind instruments as the crumhorn, rackett or cornett, and early percussion, players may be forced to make their instrument; and they will, in any case, be correspondingly knowledgeable on the problems of construction as they affect the sound.

There are a number of books dealing with quite simple home-made instruments which can be used by young children. The music library which is part of a larger system will need the co-operation of colleagues here. It is for example, unlikely that the *Woodworker*, a monthly periodical published by Model and Allied Publications, Hemel Hempstead, England, will be in a music library. Music librarians may, therefore, overlook the articles on instrument construction it has contained in the last two decades which, were they all published in a collected form, would be acquired without hesitation. Fortunately there is at least one bibliography: Martin Woodrow's *Make your own musical instruments: a bibliography* Stevenage, Clover Publications 1977.

Books which give detailed instruction on the performance practice of earlier times are likely to contain many controversial statements. The performer of such music will rely more on the several treatises of the eighteenth century in particular, which are mostly available in reprint. Nevertheless, the general guidance of a work like Robert Donington's *The interpretation of early music* Faber 1974, or the earlier work of A Dolmetsch *Interpretation of music of the seventeenth and eighteenth centuries* Novello 1946, first written in 1915, is stimulating, while being read in an awareness that definitive answers to the questions raised are mostly not possible.

Orchestral music
There are, perhaps, fewer books on the conductor's technique than on instrumental techniques. Those who study this will not, in any case acquire much of it from books. They will, however, need a large library of supporting material for all the problems which face a conductor off, rather than on, the rostrum. General guides for listeners can also double for reference use; many cover the repertory in a historical context, and have been so treated in this chapter. Such details as instrumentation, movements and timings, as well as publishers and other bibliographic detail, appear in a number of works which overlap somewhat. W Altmann's *Orchester-literatur Katalog* and W Buschkötter's *Handbuch der musikalischen Konzertliteratur* are both back in print (by Hofmeister of Hofheim and de Gruyter of Berlin, respectively) after being difficult to obtain—a testimony to their usefulness. The catalogues of ASCAP *Symphonic catalog* 3rd ed, 1977, and David Daniel *Orchestral music: a source book* Metuchen, Scarecrow 1972, are useful for tracing works. The latter also gives other programme planing information, including timings, although the better known source for these, S Aronowsky's *Performing times of orchestral works* Benn 1959, is more comprehensive, but more frequently cited than found in libraries, being very expensive. Daniel's work is, therefore, the convenient one volume source for much of this information.

The voice

If there is extensive literature about instruments, that on the voice is not much less. While the manufacture of the vocal instrument is not yet documented, the range of styles and practices of singing is wide, and many teachers and performers have expressed their system of vocal training in books. The particularly personal nature of the singer's art is reflected in the number of biographies of singers that are produced and attract interest, although changing fashions determine a short useful life for many of these; the interest in such earlier singers can often be monitored by observing re-issues of their recordings. Lists of repertoire, of which B Coffin's *The singer's repertoire* New York, Scarecrow Press 1970, is the most extensive and indexes to songs in various forms will be adjuncts sought by singers, and for those who listen there are many discussions of the 'concert guide' type. Language problems for singers are dealt with amongst others again by Coffin, and for those who listen to lieder, but whose German is limited, the *Penguin book of lieder* edited and translated by S S Prawer 1964, gives alongside the original a close translation, so that both may be followed in performance.

The combination of voices, and the problems those who deal with choirs face, have their literature; and, while secular choirs are dealt with, it is not surprising that the church choir has been covered in special detail and frequency. Again, changing taste will have rendered many older works less useful; and the variety of liturgical pride and prejudice renders some works too specific for more than a limited use. Church music as a part of music history is well covered in the general works, and also specifically. As a start on understanding the situation of the present practitioner one may consult Lionel Dakers's *A handbook of parish music* Oxford, Mowbrays 1976, in which the background of post-liturgical-reform Anglicanism, while evident, is not unduly prominent, and much is of wider application. The book has both further reading lists and lists of music which the librarian will note.

Opera has a particular fascination and a wide following, at one extreme of which are those whose sole musical contact seems to be Verdi or Wagner. Their insistent demands will, fortunately, often be for items that would be acquired

73

anyway, but are made as the publisher's first announcement appears. Books on individual styles and composers are numerous; less so are those which attempt a balanced survey of the field as a whole: Donald Grout's *A history of opera* Columbia University Press 1966, is a basic history, while P H Lang's *The experience of opera* Faber 1973, and Joseph Kerman's *Opera as drama* New York, Vintage 1956, discuss the nature of the operatic experience. Among the many handbooks of opera plots, Kobbé is still the standard (the expansion, *Kobbé's complete opera book* 9th ed, Putnam 1976, is scarcely necessary as this shares with Grove the distinction of being a work universally known by one word) and modern opera and operetta have similar guides.

Reference works
A collection of dictionaries and encyclopedias, bibliographies and discographies, catalogues and indexes, will be at the core of almost all music libraries; since, even in the rare cases where information work with the library user is not undertaken, they are invaluable tools for the librarian in the control of the other material being considered.

Although a dictionary is really a list of definitions of words, and an encyclopedia explains at greater length the ideas they express, there is no distinction in practice. The best known example, at least in the English speaking world, is Grove whose title begins 'Dictionary.....' despite the views of lexicographers. This work has been always found generally in music libraries. It was criticised as both chauvinist and dated on the appearance of the fifth edition in 1954, and the lack of an index is infuriating. Nevertheless, many articles are excellent summaries of their topic. How many libraries will be able to afford the imminent sixth edition remains to be seen, but its appearance must be a landmark in the literature of music. Earlier editions should not be discarded; the second in particular (published 1904-10) has much information on nineteenth century English music not available elsewhere.

The earliest multivolume or large volume surveys of music in this form are now items of historical interest; the curious may consult the first, Johannes Tinctorus's *Terminae musicae definitorum*, first published around 1470, in an edition (with English translation) published in New York by Free Press in 1963. The modern appearances of the genre began in the latter half of the last century, and the works of Fétis and Riemann are consulted today, the latter in much later editions, the former for its biographical information. The biographical dictionaries first consulted today are Theodore Baker's *Baker's biographical dictionary of music and musicians* New York, Schirmer 1958 (with a supplement published in 1965) and Oscar Thomson's *The international cyclopaedia of music and musicians* New York, Dodd, Mead; London, Dent 1975, while in single volume works dealing with musical terms include Willi Apel's *Harvard dictionary of music* Cambridge, Mass, Harvard University Press; London, Heinemann 1970, and the slighter publications of Dent's *Everyman* series and Penguin, which will be fairly universally found. Much valued by music lovers is Percy Scholes's *Oxford companion to music* 10th ed, Oxford University Press 1970.

Those larger libraries which can afford the multivolume works may have, besides Grove, the work known in English as MGG from the title *Die Musik in Geschichte und Gegenwart*, edited by F Blume, Kassel, Bärenreiter 1949-67 which, while not unnaturally dealing especially with the German musicians, is wider in coverage, and more recent than the current (fifth edition) Grove. Most articles on composers have extensive bibliographies covering both works and criticism, which the non-German speaking reader will learn to unravel if patient, since the layout is very crammed. France and Italy are covered in the publications of Larousse and Ricordi respectively, which will, if available, clearly be first recourse for their own national composers.

Other dictionaries cover more limited aspects of music; one example which is generally available is Walter Cobbett's *Cyclopedic survey of chamber music*, and hymnology and opera are covered in other similar works. All of these will give factual information in the briefest form, and the larger will give judgments which, in the case of compilations, should embody the conclusions of one who has become especially knowledgeable in the field, and may be relied on as

75

both sound and representing the consensus of scholarship. New or controversial theories are, therefore, not generally found in reference works.

—Directories

The librarian will depend on a number of directories covering people and organisations as well as places, and especially the more local ones. The *International who's who and musician's directory* has, in the eighth edition 1977, published in Cambridge, moved the word international to the head of the title; there is still a larger coverage of Britons than others. *The British music yearbook* has, on the other hand, restricted its scope nationally, and from 1979 will be published by Black. Rita Benton has covered music libraries of 'research' status in the *IAML directory of music research libraries*, whose three volumes cover most of the USA, Canada and Europe; while almost all library music collections in Britain are covered in Maureen Long's *Music in British libraries* Library Association 1971. These should become familiar to all who work in music libraries, and will lead to the large quantity of smaller, specialist works in various areas of music and covering locations sometimes as small as a single town, required by one's clientele.

—Bibliographies

Bibliographies are a feature of some encyclopedic works; they are also a significant genre in themselves. Music bibliographies may cover aspects of the literature on music, or of music itself. As a guide to the former, Duckles and Davies have already been referred to (p60), and the merest glance at either will indicate the range of specific topics covered. All such works date more or less quickly: some bibliographies cover areas of vigorous acticity, others those in which little new material is appearing. The usefulness of a bibliography in the former case especially is increased if its coverage includes articles in periodicals as well as books. For most purposes, the amount of bibliographic detail is limited to that necessary to find the item—a simple imprint and date— though some indication of the size of the work is useful, and critical annotation can save wasted time. Since much new material of interest appears in periodical articles, a bibliography which includes them is especially noteworthy. Sometimes major reference sources are published as part of a periodical issue. *Musical quarterly* published a survey of contemporary music in Europe as the issue for January 1965, which remains such a source (it was however, reprinted as a monograph); the Royal Musical Association's *Research chronicle* includes such things as Paul Doe's list of research projects at British universities (number 3, 1963) and sources on plate numbers and thematic catalogues, to give two other examples, began as periodical articles.

Since not all are reprinted, it may be worth keeping a special index of such sources, by subject, as part of the subject catalogue or separately. All writings on music which appear in periodical articles are indexed in the two general music periodical indexes *Music index* Detroit, Information Service Inc, 1949-   and *RILM*; the acronym, universally used, is from the French title of *International inventory of music literature* New York, International RILM center 1967-   . Although these are expensive, and will only be found in the more substantial music libraries, all music librarians should be aware of their content and coverage. Strictly speaking, the latter is an abstracting service rather than simply an index. The former appears monthly, the latter quarterly, and both cumulate into annual volumes. Coverage is much quicker now than formerly in both cases, thus abating a criticism which appeared in many earlier reviews. In 1975, both were covering some 300 periodical titles in varying detail. Older established than either, but rarely found in libraries in English speaking countries, is *Bibliographie des Musikschrifttums* Leipzig, Frankfurt am Main, Hofmeister, 1936-9, 1950-   with some emphasis on German scholarly items. All of these sources are to some extent complementary, as well as overlapping substantially.

Bibliographies of music itself may be thought of as either current or retrospective. The former becomes the latter all too quickly, as much music goes out of print within a year or two of publication; but, nevertheless, most music libraries will have substantial representation of current listings.

National bibliographies attempt to list the music newly published in the country. Given the international nature of music and the multi-national nature of most libraries' holdings, this approach is less helpful than with books, where it is well established. A list of the accessions of a national library may be more to the point, as is acknowledged in the USA, where the *Library of Congress catalog of music and phonorecords* is such a list. The *British catalogue of music* is, on the other hand, restricted to material deposited with the British Library under legal deposit legislation; and the complementary *Catalogue of printed music in the British Library: accessions* is not generally available. Both appear annually, listing works catalogued during the year, without cumulations. Furthermore, they follow different codes of cataloguing. Since the responsible authorities were merged in the British Library in 1973, this somewhat unsatisfactory situation has been under review. Other national listings are produced, both by national libraries and by national music centres, who often produce other material aimed at promoting the contemporary music of their countries.

Some libraries holdings are so substantial that their catalogues, where published, amount to bibliographies. The BBC music library, in London, has to date published catalogues of all but its orchestral music (this deficiency is to be made good during 1980) and is notable for its emphasis on music intended for performance. Another substantial collection with a published catalogue is that of the New York Public Library, while in the specialist field of orchestral material the *Catalogue of the Edwin A Fleischer music collection*, in the Free library of Philadelphia (second edition 1965), regrettably out of print with a new edition promised, is invaluable if it can be found. Earlier published music is covered in a number of great libraries, some of which have produced catalogues of collections of special interest: the Paul Hirsch collection, whose catalogue was published when in private hands, and then again in briefer form after acquisition by the British Museum; and the Kings library, again in that institution, are examples.

No music bibliography on the scale of F Pazdírek *Universal-Handbuch der Musikliteratur* Vienna, Pazdírek 1904-10 reprinted by F Knuf 1966, attempting such wide coverage from one author has been seen since, nor is likely to be. It lists over half a million pieces of music then in print, and is still a useful source. Most larger British music libraries, and many others, will have Edith Schnapper's *British union catalogue of early music printed before the year 1801* London, Butterworth 1957, (now from Blackwell, Oxford) a valuable bibliography even though some locations are out of date. The newer and larger *Repertoire internationale des sources musicales,* generally known as *RISM* (the title is also cited in English) will on completion supersede this, and the work by Robert Eitner, *Bibliographie der Musik-Sammelwerke des XVI and XVII Jahrhunderts,* reprinted by Olms in 1963, whose ten volumes are only found in some larger libraries. *RISM* should be examined carefully, since it covers several areas of printed and manuscript music and writings on music; the publishers, Henle and Bärenreiter, of Munich, have issued detailed statements and the project has been reviewed in several journals.

The user of bibliographies of printed music should be warned that any statement of the publisher or agent from whom an item is available is only reliable in the country of the compiler at the time of writing. Agencies vary from country to country, and change hands from time to time.

Returning to current material, we may note that useful bibliographic listings appear in a number of periodicals. *Fontes artis musicae* regularly publishes 'listes selectives' by country, while *Notes* has listings compiled by those with access to the Library of Congress's substantial intake. The listings in some other periodicals, which often carry reviews, are frequently well behind publication.

Several music retailers publish listings of music, the availability of which varies: that of Otto Harrassowitz of Wiesbaden in West Germany is available only as part of a purchasing programme. Its coverage is very comprehensive, and entries are to AACR standards. In Britain, Blackwell's of Oxford have produced listings under the title *New music in Britain* from 1974-7, now discontinued, and to be followed by similar information in card and machine-readable form, while longer established but much more selective lists have been produced by J B Cramer in London since 1946. The Blackwell and Cramer lists are more widely available.

In spite of the foregoing, most music libraries find it necessary to collect publishers' catalogues as widely as possible. These are aimed at users other than librarians, and are usually in the form of leaflets covering music for various media or purposes. The complete list in composer order is a rare (and to the librarian, pleasant) exception.

Dealers in second hand music generally sell through catalogues, which are usually available to all prospective purchasers. Most of the dealers have their specialities and general 'line of country', as a perusal of their catalogues will shew. Many of these are of considerable permanent value, and considerable bibliographic expertise and research is expended on their production. Since very little music appears in *Book auction records* Folkestone, Dawson or its equivalents elsewhere, and that among much else, they are the prime source for prices and descriptions of out of print material; and they remain valuable long after their initial purpose, that of selling the dealer's wares, is accomplished. This, it may be remarked, is a speedy process; little remains unsold a week or two after the catalogues' appearance.

Most of the published work in music bibliography is made up of items dealing with a restricted field, and a majority of the listings in everyday use deals either with works for a particular medium, or by a single composer. Bibliographies of music for specific instruments or groups are listed in Bernard Brüchle's *Music bibliographies for all instruments* Munchen, Bernard Brüchle Edition 1976. Coverage of music for particular instruments in books dealing with them has been referred to (p69) as has orchestral material (p72), while for some instruments quite substantial bibliographies are available. For some reason wind instruments are better provided for than strings on an individual basis, though for the latter M K Farish's *String music in print* 2nd ed, New York, Bowker 1973, covers music currently available (in the USA) and necessarily omits many items from the earlier edition of 1965 and its supplement, which are therefore still useful in tracing such titles. Pianists now have the guide by Rezits and Deatsman referred to on p71 which gives a listing of piano music available in the USA in 1978. While current listings inevitably date quite quickly, some of these above are clearly committed to regular new editions. Although the newer titles referred to here do not of course appear, a glance at chapter six of Davies's *Musicalia* shews the range available.

In the field of vocal music, the case of song is an especial trial to the librarian since much is anonymous; and where a composer exists, the approach is still often by title. Title, in this context, may in fact be a real title, especially of an art song: *An die Musik* or *Linden Lea* but is more often the opening of the text such as, *It was a lover and his lass* or *Swing low, sweet chariot*; while for a song with verse and refrain it is frequently the opening of the refrain. *When Britain first at heaven's command* is rarely cited and may not be recognized, but *Rule Britannia!* will be generally known. Further, songs may be grouped into collections or cycles, with a collective title. Popular song titles may be remembered in garbled form, or some important word other than the first may be quoted. This makes the keyword index in A Stecheson's *Classified song directory* Hollywood, Music Industry Press 1961, particulary useful—even if some obvious words eg 'moon', 'love', and so on have lengthy entries.

Covering a wider field of classical art song and folk song is M Sear's *Song index* Hamden, Connecticut, Shoe String Press 1966, which is particularly good at indexing variant titles. These are specifically catered for in Julian Hodgson's *Music titles in translation* Bingley 1976; Hamden, Conn, Linnet, which also goes wider than song but excludes folksongs. Composers' names are given, but no details of publications. There are lists under some useful classified headings, such as carols and sea shanties, in the publication which takes a similar approach to Sears for songs in anthologies: *Songs in collections* by Desirée de Charms and Paul Breed Detroit, Information Service 1966, and since Sears was first published in 1926, this effectively updates it along with the relevant volumes of the BBC music library catalogue, and with the song entries in the New York Public Library catalogue, where these are available. These two deal in individually published songs, as well as anthologies, mitigating somewhat the irritation resulting frequently from finding a reference in the anthology indexes to a long out of print anthology which is hopelessly unavailable. Singers interested in the repertory with performance in mind are well served by Coffin's *Singers' répertoire*, referred to above, and Noni Espina's *Répertoire for the solo voice* Metuchen, N J, Scarecrow 1977, although the librarian will find the lack of bibliographic detail irritating.

Popular songs have received attention both in simple listings: Patricia Havlice's *Popular song index* Scarecrow 1975, covers a wide range, and listing in terms of availability in the USA, and in more discursive treatment. In this category Leslie Love's *Directory of popular music* Droitwich, Peterson 1975, is a product of individual enterprise covering, besides titles of popular songs and instrumental numbers, films and musical shows, publishers in this special field, theme music associated with particular artists, and academy award winners.

Vocal music has been dealt with in three volumes which demonstrate a new trend in the compilation of lists of music in print. The publisher, Musicdata Inc, of Philadelphia, has produced a number of catalogues based on the approach of Farish's *String music in print*, and compiled by computer. The method is to enter items from publishers' catalogues; and there is, therefore, no consistency of treatment of a composer's name, or of titles. In the field of choral and vocal music, covered in three volumes *Sacred vocal music in print*, 1974 and *Secular vocal music in print*, 1974 edited by Thomas Nardone, James Nye and Mark Reznick and *Classical vocal music*, 1976 edited by Thomas Nardone alone, this causes some anomalies in arrangement: double sequences under different forms of composers' names and titles of works in particular, cause difficulty. The user will, therefore, need to bear this limitation in mind, along with the inevitable dating of the works and USA standpoint as to publishers: but will still find them an invaluable tool, and perhaps the way toward a music equivalent of *Books in print*.

Another approach to specialist bibliographies is by composer. Lists of works by composers include bibliographies of their published music—especially useful where many early editions exist and are easily confused. One such is William C Smith's *Handel: a descriptive catalogue of the early editions* Oxford, Blackwell 1970. The best known composer catalogues are devoted to listing works, irrespective of publication, often with thematic incipits. These thematic catalogues include the well-known Köchel, for Mozart, and Schmieder for Bach, whose reference numbers have become a standard for identification. Internal arrangement varies; it is sometimes chronological (as far as this order can be determined) and sometimes by instrumentation or by key. Such works have been listed in Barry Brook's *Thematic catalogues in music* Hillsdale, N Y, Pendragon Press 1972.

Listings of musical themes themselves, to enable identification of a fragment, are less frequently encountered than one might wish, and employ different ways of arranging musical motives in order, analogously to alphabetisation. Harold Barlow and Sam Morgenstern produced the two companion volumes *A Dictionary of musical themes* and *A Dictionary of vocal themes* originally in 1948 and 1950 published by Crown in New York and Benn in London (the latter now available as *A Dictionary of opera and song themes*, 1976). Here the system is that after transposition of all themes to the key of C, the letter names of the notes are filed alphabetically. These general works are obviously restricted to a limited coverage, and where similarly arranged lists are available for the whole of a composer's work this is a useful supplement. Bach's works are treated in May de Forest McAll's *Melodic index to the works of J S Bach* 2nd ed, New York, Peters 1962, which arranges themes by shape, in terms of whether pitch rises, falls or remains still, and this analysis is being pursued, using computer handling, and may produce further such listings.

Other index or catalogue-type listings cover publishers, and even musical forms. Barry Brook has produced examples of both in *The Breitkopf thematic catalogue* Dover 1966, an edition of catalogues, with thematic incipits, first issued between 1762 and 1787 by a publisher whose composers included several of major importance, and *La symphonie française dans la seconde moitié du XVIIIe siècle* Paris University Institute of Musicology 1962.

Much printed music is issued in collected editions, both of a single composer and in the 'monument' series, which often contain many works in each volume. Two books give guidance to the contents of such editions, with indexes which allow the finding of a single work in the rather daunting row of uniform volumes which will appear on the shelf. One is Anna H Heyer's *Historical sets, collected editions and monuments of music* American Library Association 1969, the other Sydney R Charles's *A Handbook of music and music literature in sets and series* New York, Free Press; London, Collier-Macmillan 1972. They are complementary in coverage and valuable in a library which has such material; and for those who do not, they help in tracing a work requested, in order to seek a volume from such a set from elsewhere.

A good memory is an undoubted asset for a librarian. Those students of a systematic turn of mind, or who have poor memories, may prefer to make a card index—not a catalogue—with minimum bibliographic details but notes on contents. If the student is to have much to do with music, he will find this more valuable in the long run than dependence on the pamphlet-style stock list. Nor should one begin from such a highly selective listing—which is really intended to convey music librarians' experience and judgment to those who must form a collection as quickly and easily as possible. For all the limitations of any selection, this is a justifiable exercise; two such pamphlets are the *IAML international basic list of literature on music* Netherlands Bibliotheck en Lectuur Centrum 1975, and the specifically British *Introduction to music* 1975, in the Library Association Public Libraries Group *Readers guide series* which is more a librarian's tool than a reader's, I believe; there is no text. Readers are more likely to prefer such a text (as in Davies's *Musicalia*) so the general reader for whom the latter is too detailed, will prefer something like E T Bryant's *Music* 1965, in Bingley's *Reader's guide series*, whose approach has not dated although some details clearly have.

FIVE

LITERATURE OF MUSIC: PERIODICALS

MUSIC periodicals have increased substantially in number and range in the last few decades, and especially the more scholarly work in music is often first reported in this form. While the situation is not quite as acute as in the sciences, much new material is therefore only available in periodical publications. At the same time, there is a tradition of popular writing for the music-going public, especially criticism, going back to Schumann, Berlioz and Hanslick amongst the best known names in Europe in the nineteenth century; and after Bernard Shaw, Ernest Newman, Eric Blom and the current generation in England have kept up the standards of critical report and opinion.

The survey of periodical publishing in *Grove 5*, by A H King, remains the best introduction in English, though the list of periodicals, even as amended in the *Supplementary volume*, is naturally now dated. The reader with German can turn to the equivalent under *Zeitschriften* in *MGG*, by Imogen Fellinger, with an extremely comprehensive listing of titles arranged by country. The same author's *Verzeichnis der Musikzeitschriften des 19 Jahrhunderts* Regensburg, Bosse 1969, has more detailed information on a field which was a source for much music, as well as writing on the subject. *Grove 6* will have an article by the same author. As far as tracing individual titles is concerned, current information appears in the general lists of periodicals, especially *Ulrich's international periodicals directory* which has a subject breakdown (see the headings *Music*, and *Sound recording and reproduction*). *Willing's press guide* and the *British union-catalogue of periodicals* will also help to trace titles, and the latter, albeit somewhat dated, gives for the British librarian a chance to locate a copy, much traffic in periodical articles taking place in the form of photocopies from one library to another.

The indexing and abstracting journals *Music index* and *RILM* have been referred to (p77). Again these point to the fact that the retrieval need for the librarian centres around the single article more frequently than the whole issue. A more comprehensive union list of British holdings of music periodicals is now under compilation by Anthony Hodges, filling a need recognized in the abortive project of Garrett and Sheard referred to in some sources.

Most music libraries will subscribe to a range of current periodicals, and retain some file copies of earlier issues. In the latter respect, the need for co-operation based on awareness of other libraries' holdings is made increasingly evident, both by the ease of transmission of photocopied articles referred to and the increasing expense of binding and storing large runs of back numbers. This is somewhat mitigated by the availability of some periodicals in both microfilm and microfiche on the commercial market. It is possible to make full-size prints on paper from frames of both. While the life of microforms is said to be limited, the technical problems are being overcome; and for all but material of archival significance the advantages will surely force an increasing use of the medium. At present the availability of published material is somewhat limited, and especially favours the academic interest rather than the popular. It is conceivable that larger libraries, who often have well-equipped photographic departments, could make such copies, perhaps on a co-operative basis, where titles are not available commercially.

Apart from the matters discussed at length, the librarian will value periodicals for their contribution to current awareness, especially in terms of the world of music performance, and mostly for their lists and reviews of newly-published material. While the lists of books and music are very useful, those dealing with recordings form the basic selection tool for new recordings in most libraries. The *Gramophone* has achieved a pre-eminent position in Britain in this field, aided no doubt by the fact that catalogues of records available are published under its auspices. These give reference to the date of review, so that not only can the performers, price and so on, of recordings of a work be found, but reviews compared. *Records and recording*, and *Hi-fi news* are to some extent complementary, the latter carrying reviews of equipment, while *Cassettes and cartridges* specialises in its field. The USA has the *American record guide*, which covers its (much larger) field less comprehensively, and is supplemented by a number of other periodicals which contain reviews, especially *Audio* and *Stereo review*. For wider aspects of record librarianship, apart of course from the music library periodicals, the British Institute of Recorded Sound in London publishes *Recorded sound*, and the Audio-visual groups of the Library Association and Aslib the *Audio-visual librarian*, although the latter is concerning itself less with recorded sound only.

Music librarianship
No music librarian can afford to be unaware of three periodicals covering the professional field, *Fontes artis musicae*, *Notes* and *Brio*. *Fontes*, as it is generally known, is published by the International Association of Music Libraries in Kassel, although edited in the USA. It is multilingual, and English and German articles are found most frequently, followed by French; but all articles have abstracts covering the other two of these three. Apart from substantial writings on musical and particularly musico-bibliographic matters, it covers the work of the association in the various aspects of professional development, and conference proceedings are reported, while there is extensive listing of new books, music and recordings. The book reviews, relatively few in number, are long, and cover works on relatively scholarly topics. *Notes* covers new publications more fully, and is a primary selection tool, as well as having articles of lasting use. It is the organ of the Music Library Association (of the USA) and is found perhaps more widely in public libraries than *Fontes*. *Brio*, published by the UK branch of IAML, aims at a coverage of practical topics across the range of music libraries, and carries fewer reviews, aiming particularly at works of special interest to the librarian. It also carries bibliographies as articles, and reports conferences more speedily than *Fontes*, not only at international level, but also those organised by one of the largest branches of the association. In addition, the quarterly

Musikbibliothek aktuell, published by the IAML sub-committee on reference and community services through the Deutsche Bibliotheksverband Arbeitstelle für das Bibliothekswesen in Berlin covers news of music libraries and their development especially on the continent of Europe, and is written mostly in German. The descriptions of music libraries are often illustrated.

The choice of titles to be subscribed to in a general library is made more difficult by the fact that many titles cover overlapping areas, but also include information not found elsewhere. The general periodicals may be roughly divided into the academic interest and the popular interest, while many periodicals cover special areas often, but not always, apparent from their titles. Thus *Tempo* is particularly devoted to contemporary music, *Brio* to music librarianship.

Scholarly journals
Music and Letters, which has run for nearly sixty years, while making good a claim to scholarly standards is sufficiently general in approach and non-technical in presentation to merit a place in public as well as academic libraries. Published quarterly in London, its coverage is international. This is also true of the American title most similar, *Musical quarterly*, while the British *Music review* is a younger title. A look at a few issues demonstrates the point about overlap and unique material, and many libraries stock all three. A similar continental periodical is *Musicologica*, which is multilingual and the organ of the International Musicological Society. Its articles are usually substantial and supported by references in the argument. In the USA the *Journal of the American Musicological Society* (cited frequently as *JAMS*) has a similar content, and is found widely. In Britain, the Royal Musical Association publishes its *Proceedings* annually as a collection of papers read before the association on a rather wider range of topics than musicology alone, but with the highest standards of scholarship. It also publishes a *Research chronicle*, which circulates source material varying from the substantial to the trivial and recherché, but all of which may well be vital to some research worker, without critical argument.

Ethnomusicology is a special branch of the subject which has received increasing attention, and the journal of the title *Ethnomusicology* is the standard source. Some research, as well as more popular items and news of the society's members, appears in *English dance and song*, published by the English Folk Dance and Song Society, whose annual now called *Folk music* contains research material. Research into music of the period before 1600, which has been the subject of increased interest appears in *Early music*, which covers besides musicological research, performance practice, and instrument construction, as well as giving personal news and exchanging contacts for performance. At the other end of the chronological scale *Tempo* is particularly devoted to new music, including reviews of performances as well as articles on specific works, composers and tendencies. Sometimes a new work currently receiving attention in England is covered by an analysis, such as that of Nicholas Maw's *Personae* in the June 1978 issue. Lists of works, such as the definitive list of Dallapiccola's in March 1976 are found. The German periodical *Melos* covers rather similar ground, and both index articles in the field appearing elsewhere. Some aspects of these periodicals will interest readers not engaged in research, and will therefore supplement the general interest periodicals.

Current affairs
The most venerable title in this field is *Musical times*, which has reflected opinion and taste particularly in Britain throughout the second half of the last century and all this. It still maintains some connection with church music, formerly a major element, but has widened its coverage enormously, putting off the somewhat insular and chauvinist attitudes of the early part of the century. It now includes a number of scholarly articles, as well as news of current events. including (British) regional centres and foreign performance as well as, inevitably, London. It reviews books, music and records—in some cases rather belatedly for a monthly. Lighter in tone, copiously illustrated and dealing particularly with personalities and performance, *Music and musicians* also covers the English scene, and the newer *Classical music and album reviews*, formerly the *Classical music weekly* has still lighter

tone with gossip column style information about artists predominant. Both cover the London concert programme and are sources for other reference material of a fugitive nature.

In the USA, *Music journal* covers news and opinion, with less emphasis on performances than particular questions and problems current among musicians and music-goers. Apart from reviews, it covers competitions and festivals, especially American, the industry and the New York concert diary. The most venerable title of all however, in current reporting, has for a century and a half been *Neue Zeitschrift für Musik*, and early issues were especially associated with Schumann as a critic and writer on music. These are now available on microfilm and fiche. It is currently a useful source of information on continental concerts, festivals and other such activities, even where the language prevents the longer articles being appreciated. Many other countries have equivalent titles and these can easily be investigated if the library has a particular interest in the music of another country.

Music teaching
Two British titles are particularly devoted to this field, *Music teacher* and *Music in education*. The former is especially useful to the instrumental teacher, especially of the piano, and covers examination pieces, as well as more general matters of performance. The latter deals especially with school music making and teaching. Both review new books, music and records of interest to music teachers. In the USA the coverage of teaching aspects is wider, as is the case in the books on the subject. Three titles may represent the general approach. At the popular end, and dealing particularly with private instrumental teaching, especially of the piano, is the *American music teacher*, with coverage of examinations and competitions as well as the proceedings of its sponsoring society. The *Music educators' journal* again covers primarily the teaching of performing skills, both in individual and more formal class situations, and activities in music conservatories are well covered. Academic work on music education has the *Journal of research in music education*, which is a scholarly publication, with regular bibliographical lists on particular topics.

Instruments

Music teachers will also have an interest in the periodicals devoted to instruments. The *Instrumentalist* is particularly useful, with much practical material, and is widely available in the USA. It can be found less frequently in Britain, unfortunately so, since much of its material is equally applicable outside the USA; and the same is true of a number of monographs which have been published by the Instrumentalist Company. There are a number of titles devoted to special areas of instrumental performance and teaching, of which the *Strad* is quite explicit in its subtitle: *A monthly journal for professionals and amateurs of all stringed instruments played with the bow*, and is a standard. How far the library can go in providing these is a matter of circumstances; the selection is wide and details are readily available. A special case, perhaps, is the organ, since performance on the instrument is nearly always allied with church music. It has a literature larger than most instruments, and *The organ* (London), *L'orgue* (Paris) and *Diapason* (Chicago) are devoted to the practice of building and playing in the manner particularly associated with the respective national traditions, while most of the church music periodicals reflect a denominational bias. The Royal School of Church Music has made a determined effort to concern itself more widely than its Anglican origins, and its *Church music quarterly* reflects this, while an annual, *English church music* is a collection of scholarly essays. The Roman Catholic churches in England have *Music and liturgy*. Both cover a good deal of news of events, courses and new publications as well as having longer articles on particular subjects.

Although very few periodicals aim at the singer per se, opera has a number, as well as being covered in most of the general titles dealing in current events. *Opera*, published in London, and *Opera news*, in New York, both deal principally with current productions on an international scale, but with particular emphasis on their capitals. Longer and historical articles appear, but current work and the personalities in it form the chief interest. Germany has many opera houses of long tradition, and *Opernwelt* is a lavish production filling a similar role to those mentioned above.

91

Popular music

Few libraries attempt much coverage of this field in periodicals, though much source material is thereby missed. Popular song of pre-war years was similarly ignored, and sources are now scarce, and public libraries at least have some duty to the large clientèle for the subject. Titles from outside one's own country are difficult to obtain; how many British libraries have *Billboard*, the original standard US periodical in this field? The chart listings alone (starting in 1937) are a basic source, and there is much other information on personalities. *Record world* is aimed at the US trade. In Britain, *New musical express* and *Melody maker* deal with the rock and pop scene, the former rather more widely, the latter specifically covering the current chart material. *Jazz journal international*, and *Black music and jazz review*, the former strictly on jazz, the latter covering jazz less deeply, but dealing with soul and reggae, are widely distributed throughout the UK and North America, and give coverage of these fields which are somewhat neglected in many libraries.

SIX

LIBRARY ORGANISATION AND ROUTINES:
PROCESSING

ALL OF THE housekeeping routines of the music library
have much in common with the practices followed in general
librarianship, and are well documented. Where a music library is a part of a larger library system, they may be more or
less integrated with the workings of that system. This will
alter the emphasis, and while the 'independent' music library
must be managed as a self-contained unit, the department
may be more efficient if some functions are carried out elsewhere. Nevertheless, the specialist will need to have constantly in mind the degree of success with which these tasks
are performed in relation to the needs of the music library
users.

There is also a notable move toward co-operation between
library authorities in some of these areas. Two main reasons
can be noted. First, many of the books libraries acquire are
obtained at similar times, often soon after publication, and
therefore they are dealt with in much the same way at much
the same time by a number of libraries. There is, therefore,
much duplication of effort. Secondly, the processes involved,
especially cataloguing, are amenable to the use of the computer to handle the large quantities of data. The capital
outlay is heavy, and one solution has been to share it among
a consortium of libraries.

We can see, therefore, two approaches, often working simultaneously—the centralised and the co-operative. In the
first, a central agency performs the task, definitively it is
hoped, and the result is conveyed to libraries, usually on a
simple commercial basis. The earliest general application of
the principle was the catalogue card service of the Library
of Congress in the USA which commenced in 1901. The

British national bibliography began a similar service in 1956. It should be noted that, while the LC service includes music, the *British catalogue of music* (that part of the BNB which deals with printed music) was forced to abandon a card service for lack of support. Co-operative cataloguing has come to the fore with the use of the computer, and in order to supplement the central services now provided in machine readable form as the MARC service, since this can never cover all the intake of a library. Neither the British Library (as successor to the BNB) nor the LC, cover music in the MARC service at the time of writing. The first co-operative to do so was BLCMP, based in Birmingham (UK), from 1972. In the USA, OCLC and BALLOTS have made such provision. While the music librarian should be aware of such developments, the decision to participate in such a co-operative will clearly be one taken elsewhere, and circumstances will quickly force a more intimate knowledge than lies within the scope of this book.

Two points need to be made, however, and will be expanded in the following discussion of cataloguing. The rationale of co-operative and centralised cataloguing is especially strong in the case of music cataloguing, which is extremely costly of staff time. However, those who design the systems are sometimes guilty of seeing the music librarian as making unnecessary problems. It is necessary to find a solution of the needs of music as an extension of the basic system which will not cause fundamental departures and difficulties if incorporated. The loss to the music library if it is not is considerable. A glance at the attenuated catalogue entries provided in some early computer produced catalogues (non-MARC) shews the problems clearly.

Apart from the technical differences needed for music, the argument is slightly different in that music libraries do not shew the same dependence on newly published items for acquisition, and so there is small correspondence between the titles acquired over the same period between two libraries. However, the total pool of available music is relatively small, and that dealt with in any quantity by libraries relatively smaller still. The objective of a centralised record for all of this is, therefore, feasible—and most worthwhile. The resources of music libraries being usually more limited than general libraries, the desirability of the MARC services being extended to music is much greater, and will grow as more libraries acquire the means to handle them.

It is now necessary to examine some of the housekeeping routines in more detail. After material has been acquired it will usually be subjected to the processing routines, principally of classification and cataloguing. While these subjects loom large in the minds of many librarians, and with good reason since they represent a heavy investment of staff time, they are aspects of a library which grow out of a consideration of how it is organised.

Library organisation
The organisation of a library is based on the principle of getting the material to the user as quickly and easily as possible. No matter how sophisticated the tools of information retrieval needed to provide for the problems of some readers, if these tools hinder others they will clearly be bad for them.

If we consider users of a music library, the approach for whatever kind of material, is not greatly different from users of other kinds of libraries: there are three groups. The first want one or more specific items, of which they have more or less sufficient detail, say the composer and title. The second want information by subject, from the short and simple: 'How many strings has a guitar?' to the complex: 'I want romantic music for clarinet and strings.' The third, which might be seen as an extension of the second, wish to browse in some larger and perhaps less well-defined area, such as 'new records,' or 'music-hall songs.'

If all or most of the enquiries were of the first kind (and all material in much the same format) then organisation would be easier. The arrangement of material in the library is a kind of classification, and indeed often follows the order of one of the established classification schemes. At the same time it is an ordering of physical objects, not of concepts, to which classification schemes are applied. The physical constraints may often dictate the layout. Thus the most basic distinction, that between musical literature and music itself, eg books about the violin and music for the violin, is

95

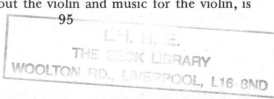

not emphasised in the best known of classification schemes, the Dewey Decimal Classification. Most music libraries will have, therefore, two sequences through the classified order on shelves—one for books and another for music. Thus some libraries, considering that the majority of users ask for a specific item, arrange their music entirely in composer order, and so the browsing approach is disadvantaged. Others, particularly in more specialist situations, have an order which is not determined by either author or subject, adding new items to the end of a sequence. Very large collections, not generally allowing their users to go straight to the shelves, may find this the most economical; but the principle of open access to shelves is rightly held to be vital in most other libraries.

Whatever layout is chosen, it is unlikely to satisfy all kinds of approaches, and the solution regularly practised has been to provide a catalogue where items are described and listed in orders different from that of the shelf. One is the catalogue in author (composer) order. This will be described later. Another approach is the subject, either in alphabetical order or in classified order. The classified catalogue generally follows the same scheme as that used for shelf arrangement, where this is employed, and this is no doubt convenient, saving some work. However, it may be questioned whether a single scheme can well serve both purposes, especially in regard to larger collections. The shelf arrangement will need to bring together broader groupings, while the classified catalogues should provide for quite detailed aspects of a subject to be examined. Thus 'opera' (vocal scores) is quite sufficiently detailed for the shelves of most collections, subdivisions by nationality or genre (opera seria, opera buffa, etc) or date, all of which have featured in some schemes, being a positive hindrance to the large majority who seek some specific opera.

It is the purpose then, of shelf arrangement, to provide the easiest access for the majority of seekers, as far as a consistent approach can be identified. Other, and more detailed or specialist approaches, are catered for via the subject catalogue. In view of the physical problems involved, some kinds of materials are often shelved apart from any sequence:

96

miniature scores (in composer order), orchestral material and collected editions, for example. Although to librarians this seems a complicated arrangement, the distinct natures of the materials make it logical to the musician. The latter is often dismayed by over-detailed classification on the shelves. Here most public libraries employ a subject arrangement for non-fiction, and thus this is the commonest in public music departments. Often this is classified according to one of the published schemes of which the Dewey Decimal Classification will be the most often met. The music library may be obliged to follow the rest of the library, and in the case of Dewey, whose music schedules have been widely criticised, this has led to much alteration and rewriting of detail in local versions, or in a more formal revision such as that drawn up by McColvin.

More recently still, a 'phoenix' revision of the Dewey class 780 has been drafted, with the approval of the editorial policy committee, and has been circulated; but at the time of writing a decision on its publication has yet to be made. It attempts to subsume within the notation of Dewey many of the advantages of the subject analysis of the scheme prepared for the *British catalogue of music* by Eric Coates, using a faceted classification approach. If the catalogue uses a classification it will need the support of a subject index. The logic of a faceted scheme such as BCM is very amenable to the production of a satisfactory chain index. This is not true of Dewey and efforts have been made to apply the preserved-context indexing system (PRECIS) developed at the British Library Bibliographic Services division to music.

Cataloguing
Many librarians are aware of music cataloguing as a problem, even if only because it is usual to refer to it in general cataloguing training. Cataloguing is a means to an end which often becomes an end in itself to those who are required to consider it. Few collections of music of any size can function without a catalogue, so one is generally provided; yet music cataloguing to average standards is a time-consuming and expensive process, and many catalogues fall short in a number of ways.

A music cataloguer requires considerable experience of music as well as training in cataloguing, and all too frequently, one of two things happens. Either music is dealt with in a general processing department, where no-one is equipped or very willing to deal with it, or it is left to the personnel of a public service department, since they have the subject knowledge and reference tools, but with no proper provision for the uninterrupted work that it demands. Often one sees staff sitting at public service counters preparing catalogue entries in between dealing with enquirers, to the detriment of both tasks. Contact with enquirers and with the catalogues is very salutary for cataloguers, but the two tasks cannot be performed at once.

Cataloguing standards

In this situation, the trend towards standardisation of practice, noticeable elsewhere, has come lately to music libraries. The first major code of practice which acknowledged the problems of music in much detail was the Library of Congress Rules for descriptive cataloguing of 1949 (recordings added in 1953). This lay behind the *Anglo-American cataloguing rules* of 1967 (AACR), whose second edition appeared in 1978, and it was only with this that a major cataloguing code of international status dealt with the problem. At much the same time, the IAML published its *Code international de la cataloguage de musique*, whose first three parts, dealing with printed music, appeared between 1957 and 1971. Although these were adopted by some specialist libraries, most music departments in larger systems were bound by the policy of the paɩ ɩt institution, and so the AACR has had the larger impact, notably in English speaking countries. At the same time, it is ambiguous in places and, even with the practice of national libraries as an authority, has left some confusion—as well as producing differing practices among those who genuinely attempt to follow it.

In deciding the questions of policy that the creation of a new catalogue poses, or re-examining the existing arrangements, the merits of standardisation of practice must then be weighed against the particular needs of those who use the library, and the speculations one may make about their knowledge of music, of foreign languages and so on. The problem is particularly difficult in a working library, where any change is traumatic. It is hardly ever possible to experiment and compare: a decision is a major step. Nor can it be implemented gradually; usually a catalogue will be closed, and a new one begun. The number and level of staff available will of course be borne in mind, as will the need for a collection of reference works readily available to them. These are especially useful in the early stages for deciding on questions of authority—forms of names in particular are often referred to the practice of Grove, or a national library catalogue, for example—until the catalogue is large enough to contain its own authority for most situations. The establishing of date is the other area where reference works are frequently necessary.

Assuming the music library is solely responsible for cataloguing its stock, the other policy question is one of the depth of cataloguing to be aimed at. Consistency is not always possible here and cataloguers should be given some guidance in terms of the length of time they should research a given item. It is all too easy for detective enthusiasm to get the better of one in the face of some knotty problem of description, and an inordinate delay will result. The processes which face a music cataloguer are basically the same as with books. The extra difficulties, though not basic, are real, and the damage done to the catalogue by not heeding them is considerable. It is not that music cataloguers are making unnecessary problems; the usefulness of the end product must be the criterion.

Catalogue entries—description
The catalogue entry consists of a body of description of the item, with a heading by which it is filed, and which enables it to be found. It is therefore convenient to divide consideration of the process into the description and the heading.

In talking of a description of the item, a question has already been begged, namely what constitutes the item, the unit to be catalogued. Is it the piece of music, or the volume in which it appears, ie the artistic unit or the bibliographic unit? This problem is at its most acute in, for example, a collection of songs by various composers. There may be a hundred in a volume. Clearly, to treat each one separately increases the workload quite considerably. Not to do so, on the other hand, may mean that a specific item will be overlooked by a seeker for it. The general practice in librarianship has been to deal with the book, the bibliographic unit. The frequency of collections in music publishing (and record making) is therefore a difficulty.

Any writing on the description of items today must acknowledge the *International standard bibliographic description* (ISBD) which has evolved out of the work done in this area in recent years. The approach to description is a common one, irrespective of the kind of material being described. Within this common framework a detailed description pattern for many forms of information has been worked out, and we are here concerned with that for printed music, ISBD (PM). This may serve as the pattern for discussing any description of music. Libraries may be obliged to follow ISBD, especially as it is embodied in AACR, or may select parts of it which seem most necessary and omit some others. There is much to be said in the latter case for following nevertheless the layout and pattern of ISBD.

It has always been basic in descriptive cataloguing to transcribe the information from the title page of a book, and in the few cases where departure from this was permitted, there grew up conventions to indicate this. Music often has no title page, or if it has, has information of equal or greater importance elsewhere; commonly there is a paper cover and inside it the music begins on the first page, with a heading over the first stave. Further, a library may bind the item in such a way that this cover is lost. The great advantage of the ISBD is that varying levels of sources are recognised, as is the fact that different sources are of different values in one kind of material from another. The information is then presented in a systematised way, and this is why it is valuable even in limited cataloguing of music to follow the same system.

Much music will have been published in a country foreign to the library, and information will appear in it in a language foreign to the catalogue user. It must be said that in all but the largest libraries the use of foreign languages in catalogue entries is likely to prove a stumbling block to many users. Many title pages of music have parallel titles in a number of languages, and transcription of them all, as prescribed in the fullest use of ISBD, gives a very cumbersome and lengthy statement which will serve little purpose. If the native language of the library is used, probably this will be selected and others omitted. In the lowest level of description, this transcription of title statement may be omitted and the uniform title (see below) relied on instead.

Some elements which are allied to the title are the statement of key and identifying numbers. Key statements are surely of little use in a foreign language and some practices involve more than translation; B flat in English is B in German, the English B being H. Here a literal transcription may well mislead. Three kinds of numbering may be noted. The first is a numbering in a series of works in the same form and medium. These are often the best known identifying element: Beethoven' fifth symphony or Bartok' sixth string quartet need nothing further to be beyond doubt. In some cases where there are many such works and the numbering was assigned by a publisher, different editions may conflict: Mozart's last piano concerto (in B flat) is number twenty-seven in most editions, but number twenty-one in some. Haydn's masses may have one of three numbering systems. Many composers also numbered their works in one series, irrespective of form, the so-called opus number. Some composers, especially more recently, applied this fairly consistently, even if perhaps omitting to number works they considered less important, or did not publish (Elgar, Schoenberg and especially Webern). Earlier composers' opus numbers were often assigned by publishers, sometimes in batches of works published together (often six or twelve). Handel's opus six concertos, or Vivaldi's opus three are thus twelve works, and one has to refer to opus six number four, for example, to identify a work. Beethoven's *Moonlight sonata* is opus twenty-seven number two.

Other composers either did not number their works at all, or allowed inconsistency and confusion to creep in. For some of these there is the third kind of numbering, that of a thematic catalogue. Most music-lovers know of Köchel's catalogue of Mozart's works, if only in the form of his numbers, eg K550 for the symphony number 40 in G minor. Schubert and Dvořák both left rather haphazard opus numbering (or their publishers did) so the wider use of Deutsch and Burghauser (the 'Köchels' of these composers respectively) is to be encouraged. However, there are still problems. Köchel's work has been revised several times since its first publication, and some numbers have been changed. This is as much of a wrench to the memory as the last five Dvořák symphonies, which were known in England as numbers one to five until the fifties, when they became five to nine on account of four hitherto little known works. The same has not happened, for example, to Mendelssohn symphonies, although earlier works than those generally called numbers one to five are known. Bruckner's early symphonies, before 'number one' have become 'number 0' and 'number 00,' which at least leaves the rest unchanged, and presumably by the same token we can be fairly sure that Haydn's 104 symphonies are safe, although others are known. That the thematic catalogue does not solve all problems is shewn too by some new ones: Kirkpatrick has replaced Longo for D Scarlatti, for example. The ultimate must be Vivaldi, whose works were published with opus numbers up to fourteen, much else remaining unpublished in his time. Between 1945 and 1974 five thematic listings had appeared, and these had provoked two concordances. The newest, that of Ryom, may well supersede them all, in which case there will be some relief.

No one system can, therefore, be used in all cases with confidence, and it may be necessary to quote more than one numbering at the same time. Many works, on the other hand, can be identified immediately without numbering: those whose title, as with a book, is simply imaginative. Most operas and choral works fall into this category, which is directly comparable with that which obtains for works of literature. In descriptive cataloguing this is often transcribed as it stands, in whatever language.

The point of a title statement in descriptive cataloguing is to identify the item that is wanted. Since it will be argued that to find such an item among others in a catalogue, a uniform or filing title is generally necessary, one might feel

the title page title, with the problems it raises, is often redundant. In limited cataloguing, if a uniform title is used,
the title page statement could be omitted without loss to the
user in the large majority of cases.

The next area is the statement of responsibility: that is,
authorship or composership in our case. This is often omitted, on the grounds that the heading will give the same information. This will require that the main heading is retained
in a subordinate position when secondary headings are
brought to the fore for entries under editors, arrangers,
librettists and so on. Otherwise one might see an entry for
example for *Pictures at an exhibition* under Ravel and assume
therefore that he composed it, rather than orchestrating
Musorgski's work. It may be simpler to leave the statement
of responsibility in the description if many entries may be
made, either on the unit card system, or in machine systems,
where the whole body of description for an item can be
reproduced under a number of headings.

The edition statement raises little special difficulty in the
case of music, except possibly for parallel statements in more
than one language. It may raise by implication the question
of the different forms of presentation of music discussed in
chapter two, since such forms as a vocal score will be prepared by someone who is effectively an arranger for the
edition, and a statement to this effect may appear. Here it
can only be transcribed, the physical description coming
later.

Statements about the publisher, often referred to as the
imprint, will follow. In the rather complicated world of
music publishing, a number of houses are agents for others in
other countries, and this may be reflected in imprint statements on their works. However, such commercial arrangements may change from time to time. The cataloguer must
therefore be sure of the situation in respect of any item
before making statements about publisher and distributor if
the information is not to mislead, particularly in countries
other than his own.

The problems of dating the publication of music have been
referred to in chapter two, in the context of earlier music,
but arise in much the same way in music of the last few
decades. If there is information anywhere in the music on the

point, it should be conveyed, its status being made clear. Title page date, copyright date and preface date all mean something rather different, of course. If there is no statement at all, most codes require some estimated or approximate date to be provided. Too precise an estimate may mislead, but a wide span may be so unhelpful as to be a waste of time. Most cataloguers, handling everyday modern acquisitions, cannot afford the time for lengthy research given the frequency with which the problem occurs in music, and should be discouraged from doing so.

The physical description is of particular importance in music, and the layout of the entry in whatever form is chosen for the catalogue should give it prominence, probably more than is generally given the collation statement in book catalogues. The physical description should be given in the catalogue user's language, and the cataloguer should be aware that some nuances of description are lost in translation, or simply in crossing the Atlantic: vocal score (in GB), piano score (in USA), Klavierauszug von ... (in Germany), partition chant et piano (in France) all imply nearly, but not always precisely, the same thing. Not infrequently such a statement does not appear anywhere in the document, and must be supplied by the cataloguer, who must therefore be able to recognise the different forms.

If there are parts for different instruments, it must be clear what and how many they are. For chamber works this may not be too difficult; for orchestral the simple count advised in, for example AACR, as '34 parts' may not be enough, and to specify in detail recourse to a scheme of abbreviation is necessary. The instruments are ordered as woodwind, brass percussion, strings, and figures used for the first two and the strings, in groups of four, four and five. So a set of Beethoven's fifth symphony may be expressed as '3223 2230 Timp 54231' ie, two each of flutes, oboes, clarinets and bassoons, plus a piccolo (counted with flutes) and a contrabassoon (counted with bassoons) then two horns, two trumpets, three trombones, no tuba. The only percussion is timpani, and finally the strings, in the conventional order first violins, second violins, violas, 'cellos and basses are provided for as stated (in general these parts will accommodate two players each, seated at a 'desk', ie a music stand). The basic pattern, with variation especially in the matter of less usual instruments, is standard and should be recognised by all who handle orchestral material.

The last main area of description is notes. Here further expansion of anything that has gone earlier is possible, and evidence for statements can be adduced. Two notes of particular importance in the case of music, which should be given some prominence if possible, are first a statement of the languages in which the words of a choral or vocal work appear, as there is some variation between editions in the matter, and the languages used on the title page are not necessarily those in the score. Then, if the medium of performance is not clear from other parts of the description, the voices or instruments involved should be given here.

An element which has sometimes been argued for in a description is the musical incipit, along the lines of a thematic catalogue. It is difficult to justify its inclusion by reference to cataloguing practice, but its use for identifying the piece in some cases is undeniable; one thinks for example of Handel's keyboard works where, apart from those published in his lifetime, there are a large number of miscellaneous pieces, with similar (or no) titles. In the case of songs, where several popular settings of one text exist, there is an obvious need. Perhaps this will be answered through the publication of reference sources, rather than in the catalogue, where the physical difficulties of including music notation have been the barrier.

Catalogue entries—heading

Having established the description of the item, this can be filed with others under a heading, to provide both for author approach and subject approach. Two basic patterns may be observed: in one, headings are filed in a single alphabetical sequence of authors (and composers) and statements of subject (which latter have then to be codified rather carefully in a thesaurus of subject headings). Alternatively, two separate sequences are provided, an author catalogue and a subject catalogue, and in this approach the subject catalogue is often ordered by a classification scheme rather than alphabetically. It is noticeable that the former approach, the dictionary catalogue, is the majority choice in the USA while the latter is common practice in the UK.

Filing under composer is common to both practices, and raises a few problems with music, none of which are specific to the subject, but which arise in this area perhaps more frequently. The names which are encountered come from a wide range of countries, and may indeed not originally be in the Roman alphabet. If the form of name found is taken, it may well conflict with the form found elsewhere, and some system of authority for such names will have to be set up. This may be that of a national library, or a standard work of reference. Once decided, the name will be standard for the catalogue, as always this contains its own authority as precedent, which must always be checked before proceeding to deal with any new work. The inclusion of dates is intended to separate two individuals of the same name, and the argument that this gives historical information about the work is clearly true, although the real cost of providing what is essentially subject information at this point should be clearly assessed. Transliteration is a particularly thorny problem: here systematic treatment requires the use of a standard practice embodied in one of the codes for such conversion, but a number (as small as possible) of exceptions may have to be countenanced in the face of very well established usage. The English speaking world has, so far at any rate resisted the 'correct' initial 'Ch' in the case of Tchaikovsky quite clearly, and Cui in any other form might surprise or even annoy, even though this name is a Cyrillic version of the French 'Queilly', and the latter might therefore seem logical. So much Russian music has been published in Germany and France, whose practice differs radically from English in this matter, that a multiplicity of forms exists.

The traditional practice of regarding one entry as 'main' and others as subordinate, or 'added' entries has caused much sterile argument over precedence in the case of arrangements and transcriptions, and librettists. In these cases there should clearly be an entry under both individuals who have played some part in the creation of the work. Variant forms of name not used should be the subject of cross-reference.

106

—Uniform title

A further part of the heading which assumes a special importance in the case of music is the filing or uniform title, to use
the general terms. Since many 'classical' composers were
prolific, the number of entries filed under one heading can be
very large even in the catalogue of a small collection, and if
the order within each heading is determined by the first
words of the title as given in the description, a capricious and
unhelpful order will result.

One may, therefore, decide to classify items under types of
work, relying on this to bring together groups of items small
enough for one to be found. This is essentially a hybrid
arrangement in an alphabetically-arranged author catalogue,
and the alternative is to provide a form of title as part of the
heading which is arranged in some systematic way. Two
forms of such a title can be seen to apply to music.

The first, and simpler, is the distinctive title. This is an
imaginative title analogous to that of a literary work, and is
characteristic of operas and choral pieces, because of the
extra-musical association the plot or text brings. The problem here is usually one of language, where several forms exist.
The usual rule is to have recourse to the original form, that is
the form used for the earliest publication of the work.
Apart from the obvious difficulty of establishing this in some
cases, and the need to provide for simultaneous publication
under more than one form, it is an unfortunate fact that
works are often known by other forms, especially a translated title. This question, therefore, becomes caught up in
others, also hotly debated, such as the language of performance of opera.

The filing title is a purely artificial device, and libraries
should be clear about its purpose—to assist finding the work
and to bring all copies of the work, in whatever form, together. In a single library this policy may be simpler to put
into practice; but the international aspect of music librarianship, and increasingly of bibliographic control and exchange,
has led to the logical impossibility of meeting a need for a
form best-known in all languages at once. Only a computer,
which can hold under many forms which it can associate,
putting out under one preferred form here and another

elsewhere, can solve this problem. The best compromise otherwise is probably to use an original form unless another is *much* better known (to the library in question). The cataloguer makes this judgment on behalf of the catalogue user, it must always be remembered. A slight emphasis on the 'much' leads to the useful rule of thumb that, when in doubt, the original is preferred.

Thus, in English usage, *Three part inventions* would certainly be preferred for Bach's *Sinfonien*, or *Nutcracker* for *Shchelkunchik*. On the other hand, *Cosi fan tutte* or *La vie en rose* are by common consent untranslateable, and are quoted as such by those who would claim no Italian or French. In the middle ground, it is suggested for example that, say, *Serse*, rather than *Xerxes*; *Bist du bei mir*, rather than any of the many translations; and *Ave verum corpus* would be preferred, after a short pause for thought, since many forms are regularly cited. In any case, there is little virtue in using a form which is neither original nor in the language of the library, simply because the edition to hand comes from a third country. Such forms as *Casse-noisette* should be avoided in English speaking countries.

The form of filing title which arises particularly in the case of music, has been called the conventional title. In the case of most instrumental music (and a little vocal music) of the 'classics' the title is built up of a number of elements which describe the form and instrumentation, together with numbers as described above, the key of the piece, and so on. These will vary in order and language, and the 'title' as it appears on several editions will take various forms, such as:

Piano concerto no 3 . . . .

Concerto for piano and orchestra no 3 . . . .

Third piano concerto

with some more obvious language variants beginning 'Konzert', 'Drittes', and so on, putting the piece all over the alphabet unless the filing title is used. The form is prescribed in several of the more recent cataloguing codes, and generally places the expression of form first followed by the medium and the number in series of such works next, followed by the other elements. In English usage, the English form of the various cognate expressions for form (which often derives

108

from Italian) is always used: 'Concerto' for 'concert' 'Konzert', etc; 'sonata', 'symphony', and so on. The full uniform title will then be something like:

[Concerto, piano, no 3, opus 37, C minor].

The description follows, and as suggested above, in limited cataloguing the title transcription, which will duplicate these elements, may be omitted. Care is needed to distinguish between a work with a conventional-type title which has acquired a nickname: *Jupiter, Moonlight*, and so on, and a work with a distinctive title. In the former case, the conventional title is used—the nickname may be added to the list of elements:

[Sonata, piano, no 14, opus 27 no 2, C sharp minor
    Moonlight]

with an author-title reference being made if the popularity of the nickname seems to justify it. This will then collocate the piece with its fellows, in this case the other Beethoven piano sonatas; whereas to treat those few that have nicknames differently would clearly not be helpful.

In the case of some modern works, however, a genuine hybrid seems to exist, where no numbered sequence is established and an imaginative title has been given to a piece, such as Stravinsky's *Dumbarton Oaks* concerto or Hindemith's symphony *Mathis der Maler*. These, out of convenience if not logic, may be treated as distinctive titles, in the hope that the case does not arise too often within the work of any one composer. The distinctive title is often considered unnecessary where the form used in any case and the title page statement agree. In filing it may be necessary to consider the transcription omitted in order to file correctly in the case of excerpts, which are treated as part of the main work:

[Peter Grimes. Four sea interludes]

to ensure that they file together after copies of the complete work.

The more complicated variations of this situation are dealt with in the codes. One which causes much effort, however, may be mentioned—the collection of pieces, often in arrangements, taken from various works by a composer or school, which are published often for teaching purposes. When these are not identified much time may be wasted in seeking the

the originals. It is generally of dubious value to do so; one may hope that if the originals as such are required with any frequency, then copies of the original form will be held in stock. This applies in the case both of printed music and of recordings.

A certain defensive attitude is noticeable among music librarians on cataloguing; at either extreme this leads to an exaggerated willingness to argue the minutiae or an avoidance of the problems altogether. The music library of any size, perhaps more than most other specialist libraries, cannot function adequately without a catalogue, for all the problems this entails. Although librarians rightly approach the problems from the principles of cataloguing practice generally, the guiding principle is always how to enable the user to find what is wanted.

SEVEN

LIBRARY ORGANISATION AND ROUTINES
CIRCULATION

THE BINDING of printed music constitutes a major expense in the running of a music library. It is generally issued by publishers in paper covers, and is unlikely to survive for long in circulation in this condition. Reference copies, too, shew signs of wear in a very short time.

Choice of binding styles
For all but the slightest items it must be borne in mind that the expectation of useful life is long by comparison with the book, and it is possible, therefore, to be slightly more sanguine about this expenditure. The treatment of binding is the major factor in the appearance of the shelves, a matter which is increasingly being considered seriously in libraries generally; and it is a somewhat daunting thought that the decisions made in regard to binding will be subjected to the regular gaze of all who use the library for some while to come. The dull appearance of row on row of elderly leather spines, rather worn, is an unfortunate characteristic of too many libraries—including those whose furniture and fittings shew a determined effort to get away from the heavy atmosphere which was thought appropriate for a library a few decades ago.

It is generally agreed that music should be deployed as far as possible in the same way as books, standing on shelves with the spine facing the reader. This spine is usually made to carry basic information which enables the staff to place the item correctly, and the user to find it without removing it first. Music is, unfortunately, generally large in page size, needing large boards, which means a higher charge per item for the binding, and it is relatively thin. Frequently the

111

spine lettering cannot be contained so that it is horizontal when the work is shelved and, therefore, it should run down the spine. This is the standard now generally adopted by publishers, and its general adoption in libraries will avoid the irritation arising from the need to bend the neck first one way, then the other.

It is essential that music bindings be sewn, and through the fold, not sideways through gatherings. This is to enable it to lie flat in use on the stand, and withstand repeated opening to this condition. From time to time claims are made for some new variation of the unsewn binding which relies entirely on glue for its make up. This has become popular for paperback books, and is of course significantly cheaper than a sewn binding. It is false economy for music: I have never seen an example which, in spite of claims made on its behalf, did not come apart quickly in use. Small gatherings are sometimes stapled, and this can save money on items for which a shorter life is anticipated. In the longer term, the paper, weaker at the staple, will finally tear, and the staples frequently rust.

The boards of music binding have traditionally been cloth-covered, although in the interests of a more attractive appearance the boards may be laminated, the paper covers being glued to board underneath, and a clear plastic film covering the outside. This process, which will be familiar from its wide use for books, is satisfactory if the work is of good quality. In particular, the transparent material for the outer covering has improved greatly since the process was first introduced with cellophane. However a spine will have to be supplied, since the original is rarely suitable, and will not be wide enough. This may be of cloth, in which case the spine treatment is exactly as in the case of a cloth binding (and the shelves still look drab) or a paper spine, complete with lettering to instructions, can be supplied and laminated as the boards.

Some music libraries have devised a system of colour coding the binding cloth for different kinds of material. The number of colours which can be used in practice is small and the system is, therefore, limited to broad categories of music: vocal scores, full scores, chamber music, and so on. A good

112

guiding system on the shelves can perform the same function, and avoid dull uniformity of appearance.

These general principles will guide in considering the relatively small amount of music which is available in bound form from the publisher. If this is the only form available for an edition which is needed, then the only decision is whether the binding is adequate, at least for a time, for the library's purpose. Where a choice exists, as especially in some editions of opera and choral works, the apparent saving in total cost of the bound edition, coupled with the administrative convenience, may seem attractive, but the real costs may in fact be higher than appear. The binding will usually not be of the quality and durability of a library bound volume.

Very few libraries find it economical to set up their own binderies, and usually it will be necessary to deal with a specialist firm of library binders. These will be aware of the problems of music, and are probably used to handling it, though the library's policy in binding styles must be made quite clear. A visit to the bindery to see the processes in operation will make any subsequent discussion much easier. If one is obliged to deal with a firm not used to music, the converse will probably be true, and it will be necessary to shew a supervisor a wide range of music.

It should be clear to the music librarian that in demanding attention for his special needs, he is making problems for the smooth running of a bindery, and this will be reflected in the price, either directly or in a lower discount rate or in a contract price. A solution which is attractive especially to smaller libraries is to patronise a specialist library music supplier who can arrange for binding (to library standards, as opposed to publishers' casing) before delivery. This will largely be for more popular works, and there may be limitations on the styles available, but the saving in time is considerable.

Sheet music
Very slight items, from sheet music up to one or two thin gatherings, pose a particular problem. If the item has a short expectation of life, or if it is a standard title which is

113

sure of remaining in print, it may be better not to bind it, but to replace it if necessary, particularly if the processing routine can be arranged so that the replacement does not have to receive attention such as cataloguing for a second time. The axiom of the past that all material must be bound before circulation is worth questioning here, as it has been questioned in the many libraries that lend paperback books.

There are styles of binding, and some techniques of reinforcing, that are suitable for very slight items. Single sheets, whether or not folded, can be laminated both sides in one of the newer clear plastic sheets referred to in connection with boards. This may be appropriate for anthems, partsongs and the like, and for instrumental parts; though its expense will probably not allow general use. Although initially the size of page that could be thus treated was rather restricted, many binders are equipped to deal with large sheets (maps in particular) in this manner. The traditional pamphlet binder is a folder, often of manila with or without a clear plastic front, into which the item is sewn. These may stand on a shelf, but the spine will not carry any useful information. This may be placed on the cover adjacent to the spine. It will be necessary to handle all the items on shelf when seeking one, which will be inconvenient. Such items are sometimes stored in filing cabinets of the horizontal type (the ordinary office file) or drawers made on the same principle, or in a vertical file.

Such material is, therefore, inconvenient; and it is noticeable that libraries have often not developed their stock of song sheets, partsongs and anthems—which is surely allowing convenience to lead to policy unduly. It is also a fact that where a more substantial item is produced by collecting a number of such works together, in a song album or anthem book, library provision is better. The library itself, or sometimes a retailer, may attempt to form collections of this sort from a number of similar items which may be bound together. There is, then, scope for some ingenuity in physical treatment but, it must be remembered, particularly if the librarian has had no hand in the selection of items, that durability of physical form is not the same as artistic acceptability, and the usual selection criteria should be carefully considered. Many albums of popular songs of the earlier twentieth century, for example, duplicate each other to a greater or lesser extent, and there is a noticeable upsurge of interest in the music. Few libraries collected sheet music at the time of issue, judging it both artistically and physically ephemeral, no doubt; and we should ask ourselves whether we are making similar mistakes which will only be recognised in the future.

Instrumental music parts
The most complicated area of music binding for the binder is the dealing with parts. It goes without saying that parts must be kept apart in binding, although examples of the binding of, for example, orchestral sets into a single volume turn up. Those who keep music in a library for a reason other than its subject matter (a local studies department is a common case) should be encouraged to acquire scores not parts; but if parts are obtained, the principle is valid even if performance use is not envisaged in the foreseeable future.

In the case of chamber music, where the number of parts is relatively small, the best procedure is for parts to be sewn into covers of cloth, or manila if initial cost is to be restricted. They are cut flush. These are then inserted into a pocket which, in the case of items where a piano part includes a score, can be attached to the inside of the rear board of the piano part. If all the parts are the same size, as in a string quartet, then a portfolio, which is a case made exactly as the front and back boards of a binding and incorporating one or two pockets to contain these parts is used. In all these cases the pockets should be open on the inner edge of the item. Both the portfolio and the incorporated pocket style can be lettered and then stand on the shelf in the normal way.

Larger sets of parts, including orchestral sets, may be treated in this way or if costs must be kept low, then a large envelope of manila, usually referred to as a 'bag' can be employed, at rather greater risk to the contents. These can only be lettered on the front, and although they can be shelved, the result is less convenient. Such bags are obtainable from several retailers and publishers of music, and are widely used by professional orchestras. If the cloth bound portfolio is used for orchestral material, then the full score

115

should be treated as a part, as it will not lie flat if a necessarily large pocket were incorporated.

Whatever treatment is used for works in parts, a clear list of parts contained must be provided in a prominent position, to enable the set to be checked quickly for completeness on loan and return.

Other special problems

Publishers are supplying an increasing amount of music in spiral binding, which is insufficiently durable for library use. However, it cannot be sewn, and the inner margin is often very small if the perforated portion is removed. Some publishers are prepared to supply such items in unbound sheets in such cases, but even then the assembly into gatherings, necessary before they can be sewn, is costly. Another problem is the unusual format; a number of study scores of modern works are very tall and narrow, since a number of sets of staves is repeated on each page; and, apart from being very costly to bind, they need to be stored in special elephant folio cases.

Occasionally a book on music has an accompanying record, usually in the seven inch size. This is often inserted in a slip case, which will then have to be preserved, although most circulating libraries remove them, as they wear out quickly. If the book is to be rebound, a pocket on the lines of those used for chamber music can be included in the binding.

Circulation control

All the charging systems in general use have been applied to music, and a music department will usually have to follow the practice of a library as a whole, although some are excluded when an expensive system in terms of capital outlay is incorporated into a library, if the issue rate of the music library does not justify the provision of the necessary hardware. The music librarian may need to remind those considering change, of the physical nature of all the materials loaned by the music library, including records and cassettes—the latter being one of the smallest library materials, but still capable of carrying the charging stationery associated with the established systems.

116

Independent libraries serving performing organisations, and college libraries, often need to know to whom an item is on loan at any time, while retaining records for each borrower. Apart from computer charging, which is prohibitively expensive for all but larger libraries, only the multi-part slip allows of this.

In lending libraries generally, much is made of issue statistics as a measure of the use of the library, and so in determining allocation of resources. It needs to be said that, for a given size of issue, a music library is heavy in consumption both of space and staff time. Counters must be large enough to allow scores of up to fifty centimetres in height and width, and full-size gramophone records to be handled; and storage space, not only for items awaiting re-shelving, but for items to be put to one side—for reservations, rebinding, checking as to condition and so on.

It is in terms of staff time however, that the demands are particularly onerous. All music in parts must be checked, and an orchestral set can take an appreciable time. Incomplete sets should be refused, and those who do not return sets complete should be pursued as quickly as possible. Gramophone records should be checked visually on return, and may need to be checked in play in difficult cases. Records and cassettes must be compared with the package: an obvious point, perhaps, but a high number are presented— usually inadvertently, not always—with the wrong contents, and much time is wasted if this is not picked up at this stage. Most libraries operate a policy of levying a charge for loss or damage, and this will be operated at the point of return. For much music available in sets, individual parts are not available, and the loss of one means replacement of the whole. Generally, this applies to chamber music and wind parts for orchestral material; while, usually, string parts for orchestral music are available. Levying a charge, in view of this and the high proportion of quite recent material that is difficult to replace, out of print and so on, is a process calling for considerable experience and knowledge.

While on the subject of circulation control it needs to be said that most music libraries find it desirable to extend some flexibility in the matter of length of loan in the case of performance materials, especially where a number of people are involved in rehearsal. If a library is to deal in this material, it seems reasonable to allow it to be used as its nature demands; and if a number are using a set this is clearly different from allowing a single borrower latitude, which easily becomes abused. The policy does, however, mean that a charging system is more complicated, and in some cases an appropriate time has to be assessed in each case on its merits.

Inter-library co-operation
The economic stringency of the last few years has brought home forcibly the need to co-operate on provision and loan of materials. This now covers not only public libraries, who have always been ready to make material available to borrowers from, or at other authorities, but increasingly to university and college libraries. These institutions, also financed from public funds, have increasingly come under pressure to make their facilities (not only libraries) more widely available so long as the immediate purpose is not prejudiced. Co-operation tends to mitigate the noticeably patchy provision of music, particularly in areas not regarded as basic; this applies especially to orchestral and vocal materials in sets. These have been provided in some areas on a subscription basis: the Edwin A Fleisher orchestral collection and Drinker library of choral music in Philadelphia have in fact become national services, as have the Henry Watson library in Manchester and the orchestral collection of Liverpool Public libraries.

So long as these collections are administered by public authorities, however, they raise questions about the validity of a subscription service in a public library context. In the face of increasing pressure on these libraries, others have built up collections, mostly still smaller but hardly different in kind, whose material is loaned free, adding to the confusion. In general, these materials, unlike single scores and parts, and of course books on music, are not loaned through the formal inter-library arrangements, but on a direct approach. Many music libraries co-operate best on personal contacts at fairly local level, and the degree of sympathy to the problems of music in the formal regional and national groupings varies considerably, but is increasing. In Britain, for example, the Lending Division of the British Library now (since 1973) applies to music the services provided in the sciences by its predecessor, in operating a national search system through libraries. It is also building a stock, which notably covers some expensive items, which smaller libraries could not economically acquire. During a similar period the London and South-East regional library grouping (LASER) have increased their provision for music, including special treatment for material in sets.

A few authorities claim self-sufficiency and the prior interest of their own public as a reason for not joining in co-operative practices. The latter is undeniable as policy; whether in practice it is really served, indeed whether self-sufficiency is practicable, were it desirable, is called into question by the reports from adjacent authorities of requests 'across the border' from the clientele of such 'self-sufficient' authorities.

Although the public library network has acknowledged the desirability of inter-lending of books and printed music for some while, most countries report very little if any such traffic in recordings. The physical problems of the gramophone record are usually given as the main discouragement, a reason which will not apply to cassettes, which are increasingly as important as discs in many libraries. Another difficulty is the differing policies as to loan. In a pioneer scheme of co-operative acquisition and loan of recordings, the Greater London Audio specialisation scheme (GLASS), where the whole field of recorded music, as well as other recorded material was divided among the partner authorities, the effect was to bring their loan policies into line—the less liberal adopting the more liberal, to the benefit of the users. Subsequently the one or two authorities who, in the face of political and economic pressure, returned to earlier practices, have again conformed. This is a striking vindication of the benefits of such a policy in 'cultural' terms, and its economic feasibility.

In the face of increased library activity, and more hiring from publishers, fewer of the independent commercial music hire libraries now exist. They operate side by side, rather

119

than in co-operation with, libraries and are still depended on by some performing groups. While the public library can only refer borrowers to them, the college and university library may use them direct, as an alternative from the publisher concerned, for works likely to be performed rarely.

Special sources of information
Both circulation and reference work are sometimes aided by special lists and indexes compiled by the library. Traditionally these have been a separate task, though in a computer-produced catalogue, either off- or on- line, these may be produced as a subset of the catalogue file. Any subject category can be seen as such; orchestral and vocal sets, if stocked, are usefully covered in lists which may be given or sold to users. Other information, especially of a local nature, such as of societies, performers seeking others to join in chamber musicmaking, publishers issuing modern composers and the contents of collections, especially of song and piano music, are examples of areas where the expense of maintaining the index is often justified by the time saved in handling enquiries.

EIGHT

STAFF OF THE MUSIC LIBRARY

THE OVERWHELMING impression given by recent writing
on the subject of the education of a music librarian is of a
formidable course of training. There is today no guarantee of
a lifetime career in a senior post in a music library, such as
would be the natural end of such a course. Without in any
way decrying professional training, one may remember that
many distinguished librarians achieved their positions without it; they had to acquire the initial background, now concentrated into formal programmes, in the course of their
work. We can, however, discern a temperament most likely
to produce success, in which organising ability is blended
with an inquisitiveness of mind. It has often been said also
that a desire to work with books is welcome, but a desire to
work with people is vital.

At the beginning of the century then there was hardly any
formalised training; it being assumed that the library techniques could be acquired in service. The more distinguished
libraries often had distinguished scholars on the staff, and
they clearly had sufficient time to pursue their scholarly
interests. Other libraries took staff of an appropriate educational standard, and these studied while carrying out the job
as best they could. Since the second world war, there has
been a great increase in formal education after schooldays
are finished, and library training has been incorporated
largely into this system, with some work in a library often an
integral part of the process. At the same time, this expansion
of further education has seen many more people studying
music at universities, and more specific areas of performance
in colleges and conservatories, and a proportion of such students have subsequently found their way to music librarianship. The trend, led today from the USA, is to expect

121

graduate-level attainments as a basis for a library career.

There are thus two streams of recruitment to music librarianship: those who, having trained in music in some form, find library work attractive (in some cases, initially at least, perhaps for lack of any other) and those who train in library work straight from school and, having some interest in music, find their way to the music department. If one were to suggest a plan for the training of music librarians, it would take two parts. The musical training would not be specific to library work, and indeed it would be good to follow the same courses of education, whether university or college (conservatory) which train those who, in the various aspects of professional music life, will be served by libraries. Some experience of music performance, ideally both instrumental and vocal, is very useful; it is not necessary to attain the higher standards, desirable though this might be in itself. Some knowledge of musical style and history across the widest areas of time and place is very desirable. The older patterns of academic training left students helpless on current popular music. The second part is the basic training in library organisation and method, 'most easily given as in concentrated form at library school, followed by practical work. Here the specialist bibliographic aspects of organisation, of music and record publishing and editions, commercially and technically, can be treated as an option during a wider study of general bibliography. It may be unfair, in the present job climate, to expect students to be committed to music librarianship at the outset of the first part of the training; the combining of the musical and the library training into a single course presupposes this, as well as denying the contact with other musicians on the same scale.

It is noticeable that there is little movement in library systems in and out of music departments where these exist, and one tends to assume a commitment to the specialisation which is unfair on those who wish to gain wide, rather than deep experience. The assistants in larger libraries come rather into the same category. For all of these, as well as to keep the formally-trained specialist up to date, especially on technical changes, the profession has realised the value of in-service training. One cannot but be aware of the wide variety of short courses and the like on offer; less obvious is the possibility, within the resources at least of most libraries, of such training informally but systematically. In a time of shortage of resources one of the most serious casualties is staff time; and especially that which enables staff to widen the knowledge and experience of their colleagues. This, and the considerable slowing down of the process of movement from one position to another, inside and outside any particular library system, is a blow to a major resource at the disposal of any library.

We often take for granted that resource which is the collective experience and knowledge of the staff, whereas the tangible resources of library materials are always evident. In a music library one often depends on staff knowledge for an answer to a problem, or a considerable speeding of the search. It was once given as a rule in reference work (and may still be) that answers from personal knowledge should always be backed up by a source. In everyday practice, however, this becomes an implicit 'so long as one can be positive of a source'. To give a rather simple example, a patron asking for the tune that goes *di-di-di-dah* is told 'Beethoven's fifth symphony'. The enquiry is over. How long would the use of reference tools take to provide the answer if one did not have someone to hand who made the process unnecessary? This kind of process, and that which checks out a 'hunch' rather than starts absolutely cold, happens time after time. The time saved is an efficient use of resources, which is what management is about. It is surely, therefore, entirely professional.

Apart from the fellow feeling which exists (quite strongly) among colleagues in libraries, there is a need for a wider grouping of kindred spirits. The professional bodies which serve libraries generally are well known, and anyone coming into library work is likely to be introduced to a national association, at least, quite quickly. The special situation of music libraries is acknowledged by the existence of one major national association and an international one. To American music librarians, the Music Library Association will need no introduction, and at least through *Notes* it is familiar to a wider audience. The pattern of geographically based meetings of groups, of special interest committees furthering a number of projects, and of regular conferences, is that of most such societies. A foreigner may be excused for judging it primarily on its publishing, and this includes many unassuming publications relied on as standard items, fulfilling specific needs which were recognised, then met, as is the practical way of such bodies.

The International Association of Music Libraries (IAML in English, AIBM in French and thus elsewhere) is a 'federation' of national groups of various sizes, each of which has a considerable measure of autonomy. Its international headquarters is based in Kassel. In the early days of the 1950's its existence depended on a few enthusiasts and some assistance from UNESCO, and in the subsequent quarter century it has become the recognised voice for this aspect of library work, through a pervasive network of contacts with other bodies and latterly through IFLA. The list of international publications, and those of the national groups, make up an impressive contribution, again on a basis on an observed need in each case. The working pattern is of a congress every third year, with meetings of the working groups in between. Most of the work of the association is channelled through these specialist groups, though as with any international body there is a problem of continuity. Policy is directed through representatives both of the national groups and of kinds of libraries. After the initial establishment and the achievement of several specific aims, the association appears to be going through a period of consolidation, and reconsideration of the ways in which its aim, of co-ordinating the development of music libraries and librarians, can best be achieved. There is still no shortage of specific targets, however, or of the will to tackle them.

FURTHER READING

This list is intended to help further study: it cannot be comprehensive. In order to keep it to a reasonable length, it is confined to items which deal with musical aspects of library science, though clearly many general items will have material of interest. Items which themselves have bibliographies are indicated with an asterisk.

GENERAL

Bradley, Carol June (ed) *Manual of music librarianship* Ann Arbor, Michigan, Music Library Association 1966.* A compendium of articles on all aspects of the subject, none available elsewhere. Some reference to the USA in matters of detail are not applicable in other countries, but most of the information and arguments are generally valid. It may not still be in print, but is widely available in libraries.

Bradley, Carol June (ed) *Reader in music librarianship* Washington Microcard Editions 1973.* An invaluable collection of articles, mostly reprinted from periodicals, with further references. Not for reading in the earliest stages of study of music librarianship, since it has, inevitably, some opinions not generally held and some wrong facts, which with experience can be seen in context. The date of writing of each article must be borne in mind. These considered, an extremely convenient collection of much essential reading.

Bryant, E T *Music librarianship* London, Clarke 1959; New York, Hafner. For some time regarded as a standard text, a new and rewritten edition of this book is imminent. The British context is a complement to the above.

125

Dove, Jack *Music libraries* London, Deutsch 1965. Rewritten from L R McColvin and H Reeves's original of 1937, much of the detail is related to British libraries of the time.

Music, libraries and instruments: Hinrichsen's eleventh music book London, Hinrichsen 1961. Papers read at the joint congress, Cambridge, 1959, of the International Association of Music Libraries and the Galpin Society. While some details have dated it contains many seminal articles.

Long, Maureen *Musicians and libraries in the United Kingdom* London, Library Association 1972.* Surveys and describes the UK scene in detail; pointing many problems valid generally, and shewing how one community tackles them, with comment.

PERIODICALS

Brio is published by the UK branch of IAML in London. *Fontes artis musicae* by IAML (from the headquarters in Kassel).

Notes is published by the Music Library Association, Washington.

These are discussed on page 87, and should be to hand for any study of the subject, as well as to practising music librarians. *Brio* published an index to vols 1 to 12 (1964-75); *Fontes* has an annual index; *Notes* indexes individual parts. All three are covered in the abstracting and indexing journals, *Music index, RILM* and *LISA (Library and information science abstracts* London, Library Association) which in addition covers *Musikbibliothek aktuell,* published in Berlin from the Deutsche Bibliotheksverband, which is less easily available, and narrower in scope. It should be consulted if possible, however.

RECORDED MUSIC

Currall, H F J *Gramophone record libraries* 2nd ed, London, Crosby Lockwood 1970.* Sponsored by IAML (UK). A comprehensive coverage of the subject.

Foreman, Lewis *Systematic discography* London, Bingley 1974.* The only work on this specialist aspect.

March, Ivan *Running a record library* Blackpool, Long Playing Record Library 1965. Out of print, but available in many libraries. Somewhat dated in details, and reflecting the pioneer spirit of the time, there is much sound practical advice in it.

Pickett, A G and Lemcoe, M M *Preservation and storage of sound recordings* Washington, Library of Congress 1959.

MUSIC LITERATURE

Davies, J H *Musicalia* 2nd ed, Oxford, Pergamon 1969. A guide to the literature in a readable continuous text.

Duckles, Vincent *Music reference and research materials* 3rd ed, Collier Macmillan 1974; New York, Free Press. A comprehensive annotated bibliography.

BIBLIOGRAPHY

Grasberger, Franz *Der Autoren-Katalog der Musikdrucke: The author catalogue of published music* London, Frankfurt, New York, Peters 1957. *IAML International code for the cataloguing of music, vol 1.* A comprehensive study of the problems as well as a manual of practice. Parallel texts in German and English.

Krummel, D W *Guide for dating early music* Hackensack, NJ, Boonin 1974; Kassel, Barenreiter.* Sponsored by IAML. Includes much material on the study of music as a physical object in the pursuit of its primary purpose.

Peacock, Alan and Weir, Ronald *The composer in the market place* London, Faber Music 1975. A study of the economics of music composition and publishing.

Redfern, Brian *Organising music in libraries* London, Bingley 1978-9; Hamden, Conn, Linnet. 2 vols. The standard text on the cataloguing and classification of music.

INDEX

This index covers references to subjects in the text, but not the reading list. Authors and titles of books and titles of periodicals are not indexed, since the coverage in chapters four and five is introductory rather than comprehensive, and is by subjects, which do appear below. Sufficient details are given in the text to enable these items to be traced in the standard bibliographies or in library catalogues. Certain names for which abbreviations are habitually used are given thus here, the expansion being given in the text.

jazz: —books 63; —periodicals 92

lending, control of 116-8
Library of Congress 42, 93-4
local material 22

MARC (machine readable cataloguing) 94-5
media: sound recordings 44, 51-5
miniature scores 26-7
music librarianship: periodicals 87
music printing 27
Music Publishers' Association
(UK) 37

names, personal: cataloguing 106
national bibliographies 78
new music: lists 79
numbering of musical works 101-2

opera: books 73-4; —periodicals
91
opus numbers 101
orchestral music (materials):
—binding 115-6; —libraries of
118; —provision policy 20;
—parts specified: cataloguing
104
orchestral music (pieces): books
72
orchestration: books 68

parts 26
perfect binding 112
performers: —books 65-6;
—periodicals 89-90
performing right 38
periodicals: —photocopying 38,
86; —reviews 86-7; —subject
coverage 87-92; tracing titles 85
planning: design 16-18
popular music: —books 63;
—periodicals 92
popular songs 36-7
printing of music 27
professional associations 123-4
psychology: books 69
public libraries 15

publicity 23
publishers and publishing 35

record numbering 45-6
recording media 44, 51-5
recordings: —acquisition 43-4;
—history of provision 42;
—made by libraries 57; —reviews 47-50, 87-8; —selection
45-50; —storage and care 52-4
reprints 27
retailers: —printed music 32, 34;
—recordings 45; —second-hand
music 40
reviews of recordings 47-50, 87-8
rudiments: books 67

scores 25-6
second-hand music 40; —catalogues 80
selection of recordings 45-50
sheet music 25, 36, 113-5
shelf arrangement 95-7
spiral binding 116
special libraries 16
stock lists 20, 46, 84
storage: —records and tapes
52-3, 55-6; —sheet music 113-5
study scores 26-7
style: books 66
suppliers see retailers

tapes: recording media 52
teaching of music: —books 69;
—periodicals 90
thematic catalogues 82-3, 102
theory: books 67
title pages 101-2
titles, difficulties of: 31-2; —songs
81
training of music librarians 13-14,
121-2
transliteration 106

uniform titles 102-3, 107, 110
unsewn binding 112
urtext editions 30

vocal scores 26
voices: books 73